Still

my

Girl

Still my Girl

By Caz May

My Girl duet Book 2

First Published 2020
ISBN

Published by Caz May

Author's Preface

Hey lovely readers!
Welcome to book two of this duet.
If you haven't read book one then go back
and grab it now before starting this one.

This story picks happens after book one and
will make a lot more sense and be a more
enjoyable read if you've read the first book.

I truly hope you enjoy the story as much I
enjoyed writing it. Please don't forget to
review when you get to end of the story.

Caz May
xx

Also by Caz May

Always Only You Series

Bk 1-Roommates Don't Kiss & Tell
Bk 2-Friends Don't Say Goodbye
Bk 3-Feelings Don't Play Fair
Bk 4-Hearts Don't Steer Us Wrong

The Mackenney Family Saga

Bk 1-Country Secrets
Bk 2-Doctor Attraction

A Holiday Romance Duet

Bk 1-Take Flight

Prologue. Chad

Walking out the door, leaving the Donaghey's my heart is shattered. Heading to the train station takes a hell of a lot of willpower when all I want to do is head back and tell Rox how I really feel about her.

But I force myself to keep walking the couple blocks to the train station to head home, to my adoptive parents' house. It'd been too long since I'd been home; too long since I even called Mama.

Sometimes I wished that the Donaghey's had adopted me and Carly, but then Rox would have been my sister, and being in love with her would be even weirder than it is already.

Thankfully, when I get to the train, it's only a short wait and the train that arrives is practically empty. Taking a seat near the window, I prop my surfboard up against the seat in front of me and put my bag at my feet.

Caz May

Gazing out the window I watch the world go by; for the hour-long journey from the city to my parents in Hurstbridge.

When I arrive it's on dusk, and I'm tired as, stifling a big yawn the moment I step off the train. Again I'm glad it's only a short walk home from the station and I push myself to walk faster to arrive before it's dark.

Ten minutes later, I'm standing at my parents front door and knock hard.

It swings open and Mama smiles at me. "Chad! What are you doing home?"

"I fucked up mama," I reply, my head down.

"Language Chad! But how dear?" she asks ushering me inside.

I follow her, looking around the home of my teenage years, noticing that nothing has changed.

I drop my stuff in the lounge room, following Mama into the kitchen where she's started making coffees.

"You look exhausted," she comments when I sit on the breakfast bar stool. "Are you eating right?"

"Yeah Mama, I am...but I um...got kicked out of uni and Cora dumped me."

Her back is turned to make the coffees, but I still hear her question clearly, "When did this happen? You should've called dear."

"A couple of months ago, and I know. I'm sorry Mama."

"A couple of months ago? Where have you been staying?"

Still my Girl

Sighing I reply softly, "With Jessie Donaghey, but he kicked me out too."

"Oh, I'm glad you're still friends. Why did he kick you out?"

Mama's eyes are digging into me, and I feel nervous to admit what happened. I feel like such a failure; a complete wanker.

"His girlfriend kissed me."

"And you kissed her back?" Mama inquires, raising her eyebrow at me.

"No, Mama, I didn't. But I um..."

"What else did you do Chad Tristan?" she asks, using my full name for maximum parental inquiry impact.

"I kissed Roxanne Donaghey."

"Oh, hun no. She's the same age as your sister."

"I know that Mama, but I love her. But she's not my girl."

"Hmm, whatever will we do with you son?" Mama asks with a laugh.

"I don't know mama. But I have to get my life together; starting tomorrow."

I stand up and she pulls me into a warm hug. I inhale her perfume—Red Door—her scent and it's comforting.

"You're always welcome here Chad darling," she says softly into my ear, before pulling back from the hug, and placing both hands on my shoulders. "But let's not tell your father all the details of your return home."

"Ok mama, thank you. I love you.

She smiles warmly, handing me my coffee and I take a sip before asking, "Where's Carly tonight?"

"At her girlfriend's place," Mama replies, raising her eyebrows as if to tell me don't ask. It certainly makes me wonder what's going on with my little sister, and I vow to be a better big brother from that second on.

"Ok, I guess I'll catch her tomorrow."

I kiss Mama on the forehead, quickly finishing my coffee and heading back to the lounge room to grab my bag and surfboard. She calls out to me, "Have you spoken to your brother lately?"

"No, why?" I ask, stopping back in the kitchen, holding my stuff awkwardly.

"No reason. He's as bad as you, not coming home and all."

"I'll be sure to kick his butt into gear then. But he's probably just busy with footy stuff."

"Yes, but I don't get why you two didn't move in together. And why you both never come home."

"You know we're not mega close Mama. But I promise I'll make the effort, for you."

"Thanks dear, I'm sure he'll appreciate that. And your father would love to see him to."

"On it, Mama. Goodnight."

"Goodnight, dear," she coos as I head down the hallway to my old bedroom, warmth and love fills me. I'm not exactly happy, but seeing that it's all the same the nostalgia is

Still my Girl

giving me a sense of hope; that's only intensified when I
see my guitar sitting against my old desk.
I vow to play it again, getting into bed in my clothes—
because I'm too tired to care—and I fall asleep thinking of
the heartbroken look on Rox's face when I left.

1. Chad

Six months later

Pinning the roommate ad up on the uni noticeboard I sigh deeply. Having to find a new roommate is incredibly frustrating, and something I honestly don't have the time for.

Getting back into my Structural engineering degree and still working at the bar has been hectic and frankly, it's kicking my arse.

My life is constantly on repeat; sleep, work at the bar, eat unhealthy food and cram uni work. I've also been doing a few sets at the bar, and tonight is one of those nights.

Walking into the uni carpark I unlock my car—my mama's Ford Fiesta that she decided I could have—and getting in I carefully reverse out to head into the peak hour traffic for the bar.

I've mainly been playing covers for my sets, but I've also been writing a few songs, playing around with some

Still my Girl

melodies and lyrics that all focus on her; my girl that I left behind.

Even now, six months after I walked out of the Donaghey's house she's still on my mind, and every day I look for her around campus and at the bar; even though she's probably not going to be at either place.

I want to text her—but don't have her number—and I doubt my ex-best mate would appreciate me asking for it either. I honestly miss them both, but I pretty much made my bed, so I have to lie in it; as shit as that is.

Arriving at the bar twenty minutes later, I park in the staff carpark in the back laneway and grab out my electric guitar from the boot; walking inside casually.

One of the female bar staff—who I can't remember the name of—greets me sweetly, "Hi gorgeous. You playing tonight? Or working the bar with me?"

"Both, playing first though."

"Nice. I'll be watching, Chad." The way she says my name is clearly flirtatious, and I feel bad that I can't remember her name, especially because we hooked up one night after work.

It was forgettable, but most sex is these days. I only really want to be with one girl and I can't have her, so I sink my dick into anyone willing.

"I'm thinking of singing something new."

"Something you wrote?" she asks, practically purring the words, and following me towards the stage at the back of the bar.

"Yeah, it's pretty personal, but I want to get a feel for it from an audience."

She steps closer to me. "You could play for me first."

She's in my personal space, and before I can think she stretches up on her tiptoes, kissing me.

I start kissing her back—but quickly break the kiss—cursing myself when I feel my phone vibrate in my pocket.

I look down at the text from an unknown number, a smile curving my lips.

Unknown: Hi, I'm interested in your room for rent. I'm a female, age 22.

Neat, friendly and desperate.

Bar chick walks away, scoffing at me and I shoot a reply to 'neat, friendly and desperate'.

Chad: Hi 'neat, friendly and desperate' It's yours if you want, and you can handle living with a nice, hot and horny guy aged 25.

Unknown: done. Add cocky to your list of qualities

Chad: done. When should I expect you?

Unknown: Wednesday at 5 pm. ok with you?

Chad: sounds sweet.

Still my Girl

No reply comes after that, and I finish setting up for my set, wondering if tonight will be the night Rox walks into the bar.

2. Roxanne

My heart is pounding like a freight train when I step up to the door of the new apartment. I'm not sure what to expect, but I'm desperate.

The other night had been the last straw with my brother. He'd had Teagan move in a couple of months ago, and they were attached at the crotch.
And this time I'd walked in on them having sex in the kitchen, my brother's bare butt on view whilst he thrust into a screaming Teagan bent over the bench.
I still can't get the image out of my mind, let alone look my brother or Teagan in the eye.

Moving in with a guy—my brothers' age—is probably a really bad idea, but I don't want to live on my own and this place is close to Uni and my best friend Nellie.
I'm hoping the guy is hot. I've tried to move on from Chad, gone out with other guys but I can't shake him.

Still my Girl

I'll probably be forever doomed to be in love with Chad Matthews, even if I never see him again.
For all I know, this new guy I'm about to shack up with will be even better looking than Chad, but I highly doubt that.

Chad is sex on legs, and just thinking about him, even after six months still makes me feel tingly all over.
I rap my knuckles on the door, and turn my gaze slightly, watching from the corner of my eye for the door to open.
It seems like forever until the door cracks open, and when it does my heart falls to the ground in shock.
I rub my eyes, taking in the sight of him in front of me, sure I'm seeing things and Chad did not just open the door wearing only grey—tight—shorts.
He leans against the door, and flashes me his signature double dimpled smirk.
"Well, well, well, I'm guessing you're 'neat, friendly and desperate'," he purrs at me chuckling.
I don't know where to look; at his abs that vibrate with his laugh or his face that I want to kiss the damn smirk off of.
"Hi Chad, or should I say hi, 'nice, hot and horny.'" I choke on the word horny because gazing over his body his horniness is clear to see in the front of his shorts.
"So, you're desperate Rox? Because I had another offer just before."
I push my hands against his chest, moaning from feeling his skin against mine again and he stumbles backwards.

"Ooo, you got feisty Rox," he declares, leaning into me and purring in my ear, "I like it."

His breath in my ear sends a shiver through me, and I feel like I'm going to melt into a puddle on the floor at his feet.

"This is a bad idea, moving in with you."

"Why? Because big brother isn't here to protect you?" he says with an odd tone that makes me angry but kinda excited.

"Um yeah, but..."

"But you're going to do it anyway?"

"Yeah, just like old times," I joke, skipping through the front door and grabbing my bags from the porch.

"Oh yeah," Chad replies laughing and taking my bags from me as he heads down the hallway.

He opens a door to me, and in the middle is a double bed neatly made up with white sheets and a Spiderman doona.

I laugh, pointing at it. "I think this is your room."

"Nah, my old roomie left his shit behind. It probably smells like sex. I didn't get a chance to wash anything."

"That's ok, I'll grab some new things tomorrow. Make this room more girly."

"Whatever floats ya boat Rox," he teases. "And by the way, you look fucking gorgeous."

Still my Girl

"Um thanks," I reply blushing and looking down at my yellow sundress.

"I'll leave you to get settled," he says softly, suddenly turning around and leaving me standing dumbfounded in the middle of the room.

I'm sure this is a very bad idea, and surely not what Jessie had in mind when he told me to find somewhere new to live, but I couldn't care less.

I'm going to make the best of living with Chad again, even if my heart completely shatters all over again.

3. Chad

My eyes are closed, but sleep is evading me. My mind is wandering to Rox sleeping in the next room.

And I can't sleep knowing that—she's in my house—so close but so far away.

I'm also wondering why she had to move out. It's possible that Teagan and Jessie decided to shack up together, but Rox could have just gotten her own place with all the dough her family has; or gone back home to her parents, since they only live an hour out of the city.

But honestly why she's here doesn't matter—the fact is— she is and I'm going to make the most of it.

Getting out of bed, I stretch a T-shirt and boxers on—telling myself that sleeping naked again is not a good idea—and I tiptoe into her room.

The door creaks when I open it and sneaking into the room, I look at her form in the bed, clutching the sheets to her neck.

Still my Girl

"Rox, are you awake?" I ask, standing at the side of the bed.

Her eyes flutter open and focus on me.

My heart skips a beat.

She looks so fucking stunning.

"Yeah. Can't sleep," she replies huskily.

"Me either," I admit sitting on the edge of her bed, my back to her.

"I'm sorry Rox," I admit, sighing deeply.

"I know Chad. But can we please not talk about it," she says sadly, sighing as well and making my heart fall.

We still haven't talked about what happened between us six months ago, and being with her is all I've thought about.

I turn to face her. "Fine Rox. You asked for it," I taunt, pulling back the sheets she's dropped from around her neck.

Grabbing her by the waist I tickle her, and she wiggles in my arms, giggling madly.

"Chad, stop, please stop," she begs, still laughing like crazy.

I slip a hand underneath her nightie—touching and tickling across her belly and scar—loving how soft her skin feels against my callous hand.

She lets out a moan, again begging me, "Chad, please."

"Please what, Rox?" I taunt flirtatiously.

Caz May

"Kiss me." Those words out of her mouth both shock and excite me.

She's in my arms, telling me to kiss her—so I do—hard.

My lips against hers again is like coming home and I climb onto the bed more, deepening the kiss and running my hands all over her body.

She kisses me back, moaning against my mouth and biting my lip, then licking it to soothe the sting.

And fuck it feels good, fucking fantastic.

My whole body is on fire, and I'm going to go up in flames from the fuel rushing through my body.

Rox kissing me is everything, and when she tears her mouth from mine suddenly pushing me off, my heart crashes against my chest.

I want to blurt out my feelings for her, but before I say a word she looks up at me doe-eyed and mutters, "We can't Chad."

Like hell, we can't. Who's going to stop us?

"Yeah, yeah," I mutter, getting up and heading back to my room. I'm cursing myself for again giving into lust but with Rox I can't help it.

She's like a hit of crack—not that I'd know—and thinking of her is my drug.

I yank my boxers down—once I'm on my bed—and fist my dick, stroking it hard and fast thinking of Rox in the next room whilst I wank, wondering if she's touching her pussy too.

As usual—when wanking and thinking about her—I come hard and way to quick. I laugh at myself, wiping my T-shirt over the cum on my stomach.

I can barely last a minute wanking and thinking about her, so if I actually get to fuck her I'll probably last thirty-seconds and Rox deserves more than that.

I want to make her come, but first, we need to talk.

4. Roxanne

Since moving in with Chad, and subsequently kissing him I've been avoiding him by heading into uni earlier, and not heading back until dark, or when he'll be at work.
I know I should face him, talk to him about how I'm feeling, but the fact that he just let me push him away again tells me all I need to know.

Sitting in the lecture theatre I'm at uni early; at my only class with Nellie.
I'm watching the door, and wave at her when she saunters in.
She rushes over, parking herself in the seat beside me.

"Hey, Roxy. You're here super early. You ok?"
"Yeah, just avoiding someone."
"Oh, Chad, right?"
"Yep," I mutter, tight lipped and popping the 'p'.
"I can't believe you moved in with him. That it was his ad for a roomie."

Still my Girl

"I know. What are the chances?" I say, shrugging my shoulders.

"It's serendipitous Roxy," Nel tells me with a sweet smile.

Her words hit me hard, and I start to sob.

She touches my arm lightly and I look up at her when she asks, "Roxy, what's wrong?"

"We um...we kissed again...the other night when I moved in."

Nellie giggles excitedly. "Really? And?" She queries, probing me for more.

"And nothing, Nel."

She huffs, shaking her head.

"So you've still got your v-card?"

"Yes," I reply, sighing.

"What are you so afraid of Roxy?"

"That he doesn't love me as much as I love him. That he'll just fuck me and dump me."

"How will you know that if you don't let him in?"

"Forget it Nel. He kissed me again, and it's not going to happen again. I pushed him away," I reply, emphasising the word 'again'.

"Fine, suit yourself, Roxanne," Nellie snaps, using my full name for maximum impact.

I feel like a fool, to innocent for my own good.

I'm holding onto my virginity for Chad because he promised to give me all my firsts, but I've been with other guys, just refraining from hitting a home run.

Caz May

I try to focus on the lecture starting, but all I can think about is kissing Chad, wondering what it would be like to sleep with him.

My knickers feel damp just thinking about going further with him. He's the only guy whose ever made me feel like I could self combust with just his eyes on me, and I need to be a big girl and make a move or I'll forever be a virgin, wondering what giving myself completely to Chad would be like.

But looking around the lecture theatre—at all the good looking guys—I think it might be better to find someone else to take my v-card away, so I'm not a fumbling idiot when I get to be with Chad; if I ever get to be with Chad again.

5. Chad

It's one of those crazy nights at work when the bar is buzzing with people downing drinks like water, and dancing like nobody is watching. There's a bachelorette party, a group of ten girls who can't stop staring at me and giggling like crazy.

One of them saunters up to the bar. Her neon pink dress is practically painted on, and her cleavage is popping out of it. She reminds me of Teagan, but honestly, her appearance does nothing for me.
She's pretty but she's—not my girl—not my Roxanne who I still can't get off my mind.
All she's done since our third kiss—since pushing me away —is avoid me, again.
I've thought about the kiss on repeat, wanked every waking second I've not been in public, including every morning in the shower and before I go to sleep every damn night. I've wanked so much, my wrist hurts and it's a surprise my hand hasn't fallen off.

27

Caz May

Bachelorette party chick awkwardly pulls up a barstool and flutters her eyelashes at me.

"Sexy, can I have another cosmo?" she slurs at me, trying to be flirtatious.

"Darling, the names Chad, and I think you've all had enough," I taunt her, waving the cleaning cloth I'm holding towards her friends who are all over each other on the dance floor.

"Please, Chad...just one more drink," she begs me, giving me cute puppy dog eyes.

And I tell myself that only the fact that she reminds me of Teagan—and doesn't look like Rox—is the reason I ask her a really stupid question.

"If I give you another drink, will you come home with me when I get off work?"

"Mmm, sounds delish." She's really drunk, I shouldn't be giving her another drink, let alone offering her sex, but I need to give my hand a break.

Quickly I make her Cosmopolitan, sliding it across the bar to her in a martini glass. She slips the stem between her fingers and lifts the glass to her lips, gulping it down and moaning.

"Mmm, yummy," she purrs, putting it down and licking her lips with her eyes locked on me.

"You're yummy Chad."

Still my Girl

"Thanks," I reply giving her a smirk and a wink. "Head back to your friends, and I'll come get you when I'm done."
She doesn't reply, just slides off the barstool, wobbling on her high heels when heading back to her friends.
At least she'll have a chance to sober up before I take her home to give my hand some relief.

An hour later, I'm dragging a drunk Greer to my car.
I'm surprised she could even speak coherently enough to tell me her name. She's all over me, kissing down my neck and over my jawline.
I'm regretting my decision to take her home, but her friends skipped out on her not long after she told them she was coming home with me.
Once we get back to my place, I drag her inside and straight to my bedroom.
Rox's bedroom door is slightly ajar, and the bathroom door is closed. I can't hear the shower running, but that doesn't mean she's not home and possibly in the bath.

Throwing Greer back on my bed, I start kissing her, thinking of Rox in the bath naked; which makes my dick hard.
Still kissing Greer—even though it's like kissing a dead fish —I slide my hand up under her tight dress, expecting to find a g-string or lacy knickers, but she's commando and she murmurs when my hand reaches her bare pussy.

29

Caz May

I break the kiss, undoing my jeans and kicking them off at my feet. Greer is watching me, admiring the view when I also yank my t-shirt off.

My dick is barely hard so standing up and slipping my boxers down I stroke it to attention, quickly grabbing a condom out of my wallet in my jeans.

Greer is still lying back on my bed, lust flashing in her eyes. I don't even know why I'm about to do this, but I'd rather fuck tonight than jerk off again.

After rolling the condom over my length I lean over her, grabbing her around the waist and forcing her to turn over onto all fours.

I don't want to see her face whilst I fuck her; so I can pretend I'm fucking Rox instead.

Scrunching up her tight dress over her hips, I slap her arse and she giggles; high pitched. I don't give her a moment's warning before I spear into hard. She tries to turn her head back to look up at me, but I snatch her blonde hair in my fist and pull back on it.

She moans loudly, rocking her hips back against mine.

It feels good, but it's just sex.

I need more, and thinking of Rox with a final thrust I come into the condom. Greer's pussy contracts around me, and pulling out and yanking the condom off I lay down beside her. She's collapsed on the bed beside me—still with her dress around her waist—and she sighs loudly.

"Wow, Chad, that was great."

Still my Girl

"Um, yeah, great," I mutter rolling over onto my side.
Yes, the sex had gotten me off but I didn't really enjoy it.
Pulling the sheets over my body my thoughts wander to
Rox and if she's home and just heard me having sex with a
skank.
And lying there in the darkness—awake—thinking about
Rox makes my dick hard again. Greer has clearly fallen
asleep—soft snoring escaping her lips—so I sneak out to
the bathroom, closing the door softly and standing against
it.
Clutching my dick I knead it hard, thinking of coming inside
Rox's sweet pussy, and within a minute I'm screaming out,
"Oh fuck, fuck, fuck!"

I slide down the door to my arse, collecting my thoughts
for a moment before I get in the shower.
I need to be with Rox, but I can't.
She's not my girl and can't be my girl.

6. Roxanne

Getting up the next day my head is pounding with a killer headache, having hardly slept because of Chad.

I'd heard him moaning and cursing out an extremely loud 'fuck' from the bathroom.

I felt a little disgusted that he couldn't even make it as far as his bedroom with the giggling—clearly drunk—girl he'd bought home. But lying awake thinking about him naked, and what it would be like to have sex with him also made me really turned on.

I'm not normally up so early—but because of Chad's dirty escapades—I'm making breakfast, a greasy fry up of bacon and eggs. I'm cracking the egg into the frypan when Chad's one-night stand comes into the kitchen. She's blonde and wearing a neon pink body-con dress that makes me want to chunder. It's hideous, and her makeup streaked all over her face makes her look like an ugly panda.

"Oh, um sorry," she says with an apologetic smile. "I didn't know anyone else lived here."

Still my Girl

"Yeah," I mutter stupidly, feeling a little angry. "And you are?"

"Um…I'm Greer. And I'm sorry if we were noisy last night. But damn."

Her words upset me. I don't like her talking about Chad that way, but I don't have a claim on him so I can't really say anything. "I wouldn't know," I confess, flipping my egg so I don't have to make eye contact with her.

"So there's nothing between you and Chad?" she asks, smiling to sweetly.

I think I should say yes—to throw her off—but I meekly reply, "No."

Regret hits me in the chest but I don't get to say anything else because Chad comes into the kitchen, only wearing boxers and a tight white T-shirt.

He looks good enough to eat, and my mouth waters.

Greer rushes over to him—and is all over him—touching him and giggling before kissing him.

He entertains her, kissing her back for a moment before pulling back and looking at me disgusted.

He mouths, *'Rox help me.'*

But I just laugh, walking out of the kitchen with my breakfast. Chad brought her home and had sex with her. He can deal with the consequences of the morning after.

I eat my breakfast in bed, scrolling through Instagram on my phone, checking to see if there's any evidence of this girl on Chad's feed, but there's only surfing pictures and Chad looking gorgeous in selfies.

It's clear she's a one night stand, and I'm a little worried that moving in with him was a bad idea, especially when I'm still hopelessly in love with him.

There's no way I'm going to be able to deal with a string of women in the house, all over him and not feel completely shattered every time I look at him.

I want the old Chad back, the boy who was my best friend when we were kids.

But I'm not the same girl anymore, and he's not that little boy.

It's a damn shame.

7. Chad

I'd avoided Rox all day, not daring to come out of my room
until I knew she'd gone to Uni. And pottering around the
house all day it felt lonely and weird without her there.
Also getting Greer to fuck off had been a helluva lot harder
than it should have been.

I'd had to make a promise to call her—with a kiss on her
lips—that made me feel like chundering.

It was a promise I have absolutely no intention of keeping
and the minute I closed the door behind her, I deleted her
number from my phone.

I'd filled my day playing guitar, and video games, before
showering and wanking to thoughts of Rox again.

I'd been an absolute delusional fool, all the time I wasted
thinking I wasn't into her when I could have been buried
inside her, and been her first; which I'm surely not.

It's just gone six pm when Rox comes home from uni whilst
I'm making dinner. She's clearly avoiding me, heading
straight to her room without even a hello.

Caz May

It makes my heart sink but I kinda deserve it.

Bringing home a girl was a dick move, and I'd told myself I'd be better, for her.

Spooning the Cajun chicken pasta into a bowl, I grab a spoon and head to her room, bowl in hand.

Her door is slightly ajar—again—and I push my hip against it to open it.

"Hey Rox, I brought you some food," I inform her softly, crossing the room towards her bed where she's sitting on top of the sheets.

The tv remote is in her hand, and she's staring at the tv mindlessly channel surfing.

"Thanks," she mutters, not looking up at me.

Putting the bowl on her bedside table, I sit on the bed, sighing and asking, "Is something wrong Rox?"

She turns to glare at me, cutting into me with her eyes.

And my heart shatters.

"What do you think Chad? You bought a girl home."

I bite my lip, the regret hitting me hard, making me stutter stupidly, "I'm sorry, but..."

"Of course you've got nothing to say," she spits at me angrily.

I know I've fucked up, and I'm not making it any better by being a blubbering idiot.

But I really don't know what I can say to make it better.

I try to open my mouth, but nothing comes out.

Still my Girl

She's still giving me dagger eyes, and all I want to do is pull her into my arms and kiss her; until all thoughts of anyone else are gone.

"Whatever," she snaps defiantly. "But you kissed me again, Chad. And I thought…"

Her voice trails off and I still can't think of anything to say. I'm to transfixed on her plump kissable lips, and also the tears that are streaking her cheeks.

I've put them there and I feel like such an arsehole.

I stand up and she quickly speaks again, "It might not have meant something to you, but it did—it does to me."

Sighing, I run a hand through my hair, turning to look back at her for a moment.

"She wasn't you," I softly mutter under my breath— walking out—not even sure if she heard me.

I slam her door behind me, heading back to the kitchen to grab some pasta and a beer.

Maybe if I drink myself into a drunken stupor my mind won't be full of thoughts of her, and the heartbroken look on her face; that I fucking put there.

I want her to be my girl, but clearly she's better off not being my girl. All I do is make her cry, and I want to make her smile and scream my name when I make her mine completely. But Rox can never be mine, can she?

8. Roxanne

For the past two weeks, Chad and I have been tiptoeing around each other, trying to ignore the tension that buzzes between us every time we're in the same room.

He's barely left my mind, and I have no idea what he's thinking or feeling.

Since the Greer encounter—he hasn't brought another girl home—and he's been home every night if he hasn't been at work.

I didn't hear him come in tonight, but I know he's home because I'm sitting on the couch wearing trackies and a long-sleeved t-shirt and my skin is covered in goosebumps, a telltale sign that he's nearby.

I'm watching a sad dog movie on tv, *'A dogs purpose'* or something. Tears are stinging my eyes and it's not even remotely sad at this point in the story.

My breath hitches when Chad comes into the lounge room —wearing black Adidas trackies and a white T-shirt— holding a giant bowl of popcorn.

Still my Girl

The sexy smirk on his face, that as usual highlights his double dimple makes my stomach flip, and against my better judgement I can't push him away tonight.
I feel a tug of attraction—like magnets—pulling us together.
"Extra butter?" I query, nodding to the bowl of popcorn.
"You know it Rox," he jeers laughing.
I pause the movie, looking straight up at him standing at the foot of the couch.
"Are we good?"
"Yeah, Rox, we're good. Scoot over."
He sits down next to me and I lean against his abs; between his legs. It feels so amazing, perfect even.
I put the movie back on, nestling into his body more.
Together we eat the popcorn—that's on my lap—and without warning Chad starts playing with my hair, running his fingers through it and plaiting bits.
His fingers feel amazing—no matter where they're touching me—and I let out a moan that makes Chad shift a little behind me.
I'm content just being with him—like old times—even though my body is on fire with his touch, and sitting between his legs.
The movie is up to a sad part and I can't hold back the tears that have been stinging my eyes anymore. Starting to sob, I take in a strangled breath and stand up, pulling away from Chad's arms around me. Even though they're

comforting, they are almost suffocating whilst watching the dog taking its last breaths.

I pause it, running to my bedroom and throwing myself face down on the bed, clutching my pillow and crying into it.

Barely a minute later Chad comes in, sitting on the bed beside me, and rubbing his hand up and down my back.

"Rox, are you ok?" He asks, leaning down towards my face. "We didn't finish the movie."

I sit up, clutching the pillow to my chest.

"I can't watch it anymore. It makes me think of Bruno."

He shifts closer to me on the bed, yanking the pillow from my arms and hugging me for a minute, letting me sob into his shoulder.

Pulling back and brushing a finger across my cheek he asks, "What happened to Bruno?"

"He…he…died…not long after you left."

"Oh, Rox, I'm so sorry. Was he unwell?" He asks, with genuine care in his tone that makes my heart thump in my chest.

"Yeah…kidney failure. But he was fifteen."

"Still, Rox. He was your dog. Losing a pet anytime is hard."

"Yeah, it still hurts."

"I bet," he replies softly, hugging me again and kissing my hair. It sends a delightful shiver through me and breaking the hug a minute later I pull him down to lay beside me.

Still my Girl

He wraps his arms around my waist, and we just lie on my bed looking at each other.

I can feel my heart thumping—loudly—in my chest, and butterflies are dancing in my stomach. This is just like old times—taking comfort in each other—but now it feels so much more intimate.

And makes me wonder if Chad honestly feels the same as I do.

9. Chad

It's been a month or so since I spent the night in Rox's bed
—after she told me about Bruno—and I'm still cursing
myself for not making her feel better with kisses.
Just seeing her so upset tugged at my heart, but having her
in my arms made me ache for her, ache to make her mine
completely.
But since that night things have shifted back to the old
times like when we were kids. And we're just living in the
same house, making small talk when we see each other.
It's killing me, and making me feel a little torn about how I
should proceed with her, wondering whether I should
make another move or just let it be, and keep pining after
like a lovesick wanker.
I've certainly been wanking—way too much—but it's not
enough now. It will never be enough.
To get me out of the funk, I've invited some friends over
for a booze up. There's music pumping through my small
house, and I'm downing a beer watching my friends
chatting and dancing in my lounge room.

Still my Girl

My foster brother Jairus comes over to where I'm leaning against the kitchen bench.

"Got any whiskey, bro?" He asks, raising his dark eyebrows.

"Yeah, top of the pantry."

He gets out the whiskey and pours some into a plastic cup, sipping it and leaning against the bench next to me.

"So which chick has got you so pussy whipped?" He asks, elbowing me in the side.

"She's not here. And I'm so not pussy whipped."

"Have you had her?"

"Nah, well, yeah, kinda. We've pashed and done a bit of touching, but that's all."

"So why are you still chasing her Chadster? Allis can't take her pretty peepers off you tonight and you look like shit."

"Um yeah, thanks," I reply with sarcasm lacing my voice. "But it's different with Rox."

He gapes at me. "Rox? As in Roxanne Donaghey?"

"Yeah, she's living with me. Some disagreement with her brother, but she won't tell me."

"God, I haven't seen her since high school. She'd be a goddess now, all grown up."

"Oh yeah," I muse thinking of Rox naked. "She's all curves. Sexy as fuck."

"Even so, man, if she's not putting out just forget about her."

I look at my brother, who's smirking like a devil and nodding towards Allis on the couch.

43

Caz May

"Go put Allis out of her misery. She's down for a pash, and then some and I'm not normally one to share but she's a good root."

Gulping down the rest of my beer, I meander over to sit next to Allis on the couch. She squirms next to me and I put an arm around her shoulder pulling her close.
I whisper in her ear, "You look hot, Allis."
She giggles, and turns to look straight at me.
She's definitely pretty, but she's not Rox and when she kisses me I feel nothing. I kiss her back, a little harder but I'm imagining kissing Rox. I can't shake her, she's always in my head.
And even though I'm kissing Allis, I know the moment Rox comes home. I hear the front door open and slam closed, and I hear Rox's gasp—which sounds kinda dirty—when she runs off towards her room.
Throwing Allis aside, she grunts, but I honestly don't care. I just want to be with Rox. Running into her room I find her lying on her bed; sniffing back tears.
Sitting next to her I try to kiss her, but she turns away from me and it's like a punch in the chest.
"I'm sorry, Rox."
"You don't have to be sorry, just go back to her. It's clear you don't want to be with me, Chad. I get it ok."
"You have no idea what I want Rox."

Still my Girl

"Yeah, because you don't show me, or tell me. Just get out and leave me alone."

I comply with her request, even though it hurts like hell. I've never felt like this when a girl has rejected me before. And I know it's only because Rox is it—she's my girl—and I have to do something to make it up to her, but firstly I'm going to give her some space to work out how she feels about me.

10. Roxanne

Stupidly I pushed Chad away—again—but seeing him pashing another girl hurt, like really hurt as though he was literally stomping on my heart. All I really want is to be with him again—take things further—but then he pushes me away by pashing yet another girl.

I shouldn't still want him, when it's clear to a blind man—despite his words—that he doesn't want me.

Surely, if he wanted me he'd make a move. He's never been one to not make his feelings obvious, except when it comes to me.

I feel like I'm doomed to pine after him unless I get my damn act together—like Nellie suggested—and make a move to flaunt myself more. It seems like such a silly idea, but I need Chad to see me; really see me.

Waking up the next day, after again seeing Chad pashing someone else I sneak out of my bedroom in only my knickers; with my arms over my chest. I'm not expecting to see Chad out of bed, but he walks in—only in tight running shorts—with his bare abs dewy from sweat.

He gulps when he looks at me.

"Morning Rox. You heading to the shower?"

"Yeah, unless you want to go first?"

"Would you mind? I'm so fucking sweaty. My balls are sticking together."

"Um, ok, but eww gross, Chad."

He pushes past me, and I almost drop my hands from my chest. He's seen me half naked before but the look in his eyes right now is telling me he's turned on. I don't dare look down at his crotch.

Standing in the bathroom door jamb, he taunts, "You could join me, Rox?"

"Um, no...I'll pass," I mutter, gulping down the lump in my throat.

He starts to strip, his fingers sliding his running shorts over his arse, and down his muscular legs.

God, he's fucking gorgeous.

I can't tear my eyes away from his body. He's wearing jocks that highlight his package, and when he slips them down his legs—with his sexy smirk on his face—I gulp, running out of the bathroom and back to my bedroom.

Caz May

I hear the water start, but not the sound of the door closing and I tell myself to breath, to not think about him naked—wet—and lathering himself with soap.

But I can't not think about him and the kisses we've shared.

Nellie's advice pops into my head, and without thinking about it—and the consequences—I head back to the bathroom.

His eyes are closed, and he's humming softly. I just stare at him for a moment—my whole body tingling—slipping my knickers down my legs, softly giggling.

Sliding open the glass door of the double shower I step in —admiring his body glistening with soap and water— grabbing his semi-hard dick in my hand, starting to stroke it. He moans, his eyes fluttering open.

"Um, fuck, Rox. What are you doing?" he asks, looking down at my hand gripping his dick for a moment before his eyes rake over my body.

"Touching you," I murmur, biting down on my lip.

"I can feel that Rox," he says oddly. "But why now?"

I run my other hand down the ridge in his abs, and he murmurs loudly, his body shaking in pleasure.

"Because seeing you with another girl made me want you," I confess.

"Oh, really? Are you wet for me, Rox?" he teases.

"Find out," I taunt.

Still my Girl

He doesn't even take a minute to process my words before he's pulling me closer, kissing me so hard I'm breathless for a moment.

His hand slides down between us, straight inside me, and I feel like I'm going to come apart with just that simple touch.

His kiss on my lips is intense, intoxicating and I've never been more turned on in my entire life.

Biting my upper lip, he pulls back a little—our lips still a breath apart—whispering, "Fuck, Rox, so wet, baby."

I can't help but let out a moan, his finger driving in and out of my pussy, and his thumb flicking my clit.

I'm stroking his dick, and he's kissing me again—hard and wanting—his moans of pleasure vibrating against my lips, driving me absolutely crazy.

I'm not completely innocent, I've kissed guys before, touched guys before, but with Chad, it feels like the first time.

And I don't want it to end, but I can feel my body ricocheting towards my climax.

Tearing my mouth from his, I bellow, "Chad, I'm going to come!"

"Oh yeah you are Rox," he teases, his forehead against mine. "And so am I."

And he does, his thick creamy load spurting out all over my hand and stomach.

"Fuck, Rox. That felt so good. You gonna come for me, baby?"

I nod, tipping my head back to give in to the pleasure that is rushing through me.

"Yes, oh god, yes," I moan, falling apart for him.

Smirking at me, he withdraws his fingers, and licks them.

"Yummy," he says with a chuckle.

I playfully smack his abs. "Not funny, Chad."

"Never said it was funny, Rox. You taste delicious, and I will taste you again."

I look up at him—at the dimpled smirk on his face—and regret hits me. Not even bothering to clean up, I rush out of the shower, grabbing a towel and running back to my bedroom.

Slamming the door behind me, I curse out loud, "Fuck, fuck, fuck!"

I've fucked up, giving into Chad again. He clearly wants nothing from me but sex, and again I fell right into his trap. And it's only because I'm hopelessly in love with him and will take whatever I can get, but I want more.

I want Chad to love me back.

11. Chad

Rox had been on some weird cloud nine since our shower fun and had been flitting around the house in her underwear—teasing me—but not letting me make any other move to be with her again.

I've practically got a permanent hard-on—blue balls times a hundred—knowing what's under her skimpy knickers and crop bras.

Knowing how her body reacts to my touch, and how amazing her kisses are doesn't help matters either. And tonight she's taunting me, making me feel like a big brother, instead of a guy she's got the hots for; who can make her come.

She's getting ready to go out—with some douche—and I'm helping her choose an outfit.

I'm sitting on her bed, scrolling through Instagram, but I look straight up at her, choking on my own damn saliva when I look at her in the outfit she comes out of her walk-in robe wearing. It's as hot as hell—a black figure-hugging dress that practically shows her pussy, it's so high on her thighs and it's a halter neck which pushes her tits up, giving her cleavage a boost.

"You can't wear that Rox," I tell her, gulping down the extra saliva from my watering mouth.

I want to strip the dress right off her, and taste her sweet pussy like I've wanted to do for weeks since our dirty time in the shower.

"Why not? It's my fave."

"That dress is asking for it."

She taunts me, a cute smile on her face, "Maybe I am."

"Yeah," I mutter, jumping up quickly hearing the doorbell.

She heads to the bathroom to finish her makeup whilst I head to the door.

Opening the door I'm faced with Rox's date. He's a waif of a guy, slightly built with jet black hair slicked back with what appears to be an entire jar of gel.

He's not good enough for Rox. And I wonder what she sees in such an ugly fucker.

I just glare at him, and he extends a hand to me which I don't shake.

"Hey, man. Is Roxy ready?"

I want to say something to get this guy to fuck off, to take Rox out myself, but instead, I snarl, "She's coming."

He shifts uncomfortably on his feet—whilst I stare him down—leaving him standing on the porch, not letting him in.

Still my Girl

"So are you her brother?" he asks, with a sinister smirk that makes me again want to make him fuck off, this time with a punch to his ugly mug. A broken nose would probably be an improvement to his ugly face.

"No, but if you hurt her you'll wish you were dead," I threaten, balling my fists for a moment before cracking my knuckles.

He has the balls to chuckle, nodding and muttering, "Noted."

It's then that Rox comes out, and she's a fucking knockout. Her hair up in a bun, her makeup light but stunning; she's absolutely fucking beautiful.

She runs to the door—all smiles—when she greets the fucker at the door she makes my heart shatter.

It's as though she's trying to make me feel like her brother; which is the last thing I want.

I want to slam the door in his ugly as fuck face and make Rox mine again; to make her see that I'm most definitely not her big brother.

12. Roxanne

The moment I come out from the bathroom and look at Chad keeping my date at arm's length at the door I feel bad —guilty even—for even accepting the date in the first place. The jealously is painted all over Chad's face—his eyes dark—and I think about turning my date away.
He's not at all attractive but seems nice enough, and he asked me out.
Giving Chad a sweet smile I kiss my date on the cheek.
"Hi Andy," I greet him sweetly.
"Hi Roxy. You look stunning," he replies with a snigger that makes me feel a little uneasy.
I look back towards Chad, and he's frowning, showing me he's clearly not happy about me going on a date.
But for all I care, he can go suck his own dick.
He hasn't shown any interest in taking me out—just interest when it comes to sex—so I'm going out, putting myself out there.

Still my Girl

"Don't wait up Chad," I coo at him, taking Andy's hand to leave.

Getting in the taxi—waiting on the curb—my phone buzzes in my clutch with a text from Chad.

Chad: Where is he taking you?
Roxy: Don't know. I'll text you later. Don't worry.

The drive to the club is quick, and I'm feeling a little anxious—out of my depth—when Andy pulls me up to the bar.

He snakes an arm around my waist, pulling me against his side possessively and winking at me. I smile back, absentmindedly gazing around the bar whilst Andy buys me a drink.

He smirks at me, giving me a kiss on the forehead—which feels odd—and hands me the drink.

"Drink up, gorgeous," he says, clinking his glass against mine.

I only take one sip, but find that it's super strong—weird and off—even for whiskey.

Pulling out of Andy's grip, I excuse myself, and head for the toilets.

"Don't be long gorgeous. I'll hold your drink for you," Andy calls back to me with the same snigger in his tone from earlier. It rubs me the wrong way and makes my heart pound in a bad way.

Caz May

Rushing into an empty cubicle I sit on the toilet, not pulling my underwear down or anything before grabbing my phone out of my clutch.

The screen looks a little blurry, but I manage to text Chad with one finger typing, whilst squinting a little.

Roxy: I don't feel good

His reply is super quick, as though he's sitting on his phone waiting for the text I promised to send.

Chad: What happened?
Roxy: I don't know. He bought me a drink

My head suddenly feels fuzzy, the vibration from his next text making my head pound.

Chad: Rox, no. Stay there. I'm coming to get you.

Yep, dizzy as fuck.
I slide down off the toilet, my back crashing against the side of the cubicle when another text comes through.

Chad: Rox? Where are you?
Roxy: Equinox.

Still my Girl

Chad: I'm coming. Stay there.

I start to type a reply—but don't send it—when my eyes close, and blackness overtakes me.
Chad is coming to save me from whatever this hell is.
He's mine, my saviour.

13. *Chad*

Throwing some clothes on, I race out the door whilst still tugging my runners on my feet.

Running to the car, I unlock it hastily, my heart racing as I gun it to the club.

I'm panicking, not knowing how much time I have, and hoping like hell that Rox is ok.

It's only a ten-minute drive to Equinox, but there's no parking out the front, which makes the panic rise in my chest more.

It's been twenty minutes since Rox text me; which could be twenty minutes too late.

Quickly I make an illegal turn, parking the car in a back street—with permit signs—before running to the club without even locking the car. The only thing that matters is getting inside and finding my girl.

Still my Girl

Entering the club, five minutes later I glance around at all the people in the club—at the bar, on the dance floor—it's crowded and loud.

I can't see Rox anywhere but spot Andy leaning against the bar, sipping on a drink.

Prowling up to him, I curse in his face, "You fucking arsehole. Where is she?"

He glares at me—a cocky grin on his butt ugly mug—like he doesn't recognise me from meeting me less than an hour ago.

"What are you saying, mate?"

"Where is Roxanne?" I yell at him.

"She's just in the bathroom," he says with a smug laugh like he doesn't give a shit about Rox.

"Right, so you're telling me she messaged me to come get her from the bathroom."

"You said it mate."

I'm seething, irate that he's so insolent and calling me his mate is laughable.

"She said her drink was really strong," I tell him.

"It was just whiskey mate. Not my fault she's a Cadbury."

Again I'm seething—balling my fists—ready to throw a punch to his face that really honestly looks like he's been dragged through the bush backwards.

"Look mate calm down. I like the girl, but she's such a prude. Won't even give a guy a kiss, so I slipped her something to make her let her guard down."

Caz May

I can't believe the words that he let slip from his lips so casually.

"So you roofied her?"

"Just gave her a pick me up. A lick of Special K."

"You motherfucking perverted prick!" I bellow at him, pushing my hands against his chest.

He slips back, chuckling. "You wanna fight me for her? Go ahead, man."

I think about fighting him—but he's not worth it—so I walk away, turning my back to him, hearing him call out, "She's not worth the trouble, anyway."

He's so fucking wrong about that.

I'd fight anyone for Rox, but he's just an arsehole not worth getting myself kicked out of the club for when my girl's life is on the line.

Pushing through the crowd to the bathroom I'm a little breathless, but the moment I find the bathroom's at the very back of the club I barge in like a crazy animal and the girls staring at their reflections in the mirrors over the sinks jump back screaming. I don't care.

Walking in further—past the girls now staring at me—I call out Rox's name.

I don't hear a response, and I'm panicking.

Turning to the girls admiring me I ask, "Did anyone see a brunette in a black dress come in?" None of them reply, just shake their heads at me.

Still my Girl

I curse under my breath, then call out, "Roxanne, are you in here, baby?"

The bathroom is silent for a moment—now the girls have cleared out—and I hear a painful moan coming from the cubical at the end.

The door is locked when I try to push it, so I stand back, hoisting my leg up karate style and I kick it in.

It crashes back against the wall, and I find Rox sitting on the floor by the toilet, her arms by her side. Her eyes are closed and she's clearly out of it.

Picking her up bridal style—carrying her out—I walk past the bar, giving Andy an evil smirk and taunting him, "She kisses me. You don't deserve a girl like Rox, but you might like the skanks in the bathroom."

Roxanne is mine, and he won't get to do to her what he had in mind. I carry her out to the car; thankful it's still parked on the street and doesn't have a fine on the windscreen.

I carefully put her in the back seat—lying her down—clipping the seatbelts over her feet and her stomach.

Getting in the driver's seat, I panic when the engine takes to long to turn over, but thankfully after a couple of minutes it roars to life and I head to the hospital.

It's only a short drive, but when we arrive she's passed out —clearly unconscious—and carrying her inside to the emergency department I wonder if Andy was telling the truth about what he gave her.

14. Roxanne

My head feels a little woozy when I open my eyes.

Glancing around I realise I'm clearly not at home but in a hospital bed.

I smile noticing Chad is sleeping in the tub chair beside the bed, his head resting on the sheets at my hips.

The smell of bleach hits my nose, and I splutter a moment before whispering, "Chad?"

He startles awake, his eyes fluttering open and shaking his head he practically yells, "Oh my god, Rox, you're awake."

He's clearly panicked and glad that I'm waking up.

I can't remember anything from the night before, after leaving home with Andy.

"What happened?" I ask, meekly, swallowing the lump down in my incredibly dry throat.

"You were roofied. Prick gave you Ketamine."

I gape at him, shocked because I have absolutely no idea what he's talking about.

"What? What the hell is that?"

Still my Girl

He takes my hand, absentmindedly rubbing his thumb over my palm. It sends an odd shiver through me.

He chuckles lightly, and says, "Basically a date rape drug on steroids Rox. You're lucky you even got to the bathroom to message me and only had a sip of the whiskey."

That's when the tears hit my eyes—sobbing tears I wipe away from my cheeks—asking Chad softly, "So he? Did he?" My voice comes out so soft I'm worried Chad didn't hear me.

"Rape you?" he says, making me gulp and close my eyes, too scared to hear the answer whilst Chad is looking at me with so much care in his eyes.

"Yeah," I mutter through my clenched teeth.

"No, the doctors checked everything last night. But fuck Rox, I thought I'd lost you," Chad declares with so much conviction I open my eyes and glare at him.

Something has changed for sure.

The look he's giving me is really sweet and caring.

"You save me Chad," I tell him squeezing his hand, about to lean forward and kiss him when the Doctor comes in before I can move and before Chad can reply.

The older male speaks a whole heap of medical jargon at me, that I honestly don't hear or understand a word of except, *'we'll get your discharge papers ready and you can be on your way.'* When the doctor leaves the room I look back at Chad who is laughing crazily, an infectious smile on his face that makes me smile as well.

"What's so funny?" I ask him, trying to give him a greasy.

"I might have told a little fib to get you seen last night," he confesses with his sexy signature smirk, that makes me highly suspicious.

"And that was?" I enquire, raising my eyebrow at him.

"That you're my fiancée," he confesses, winking at me like a devil.

Playfully I punch him, jeering, "You did not?"

"Yep, I kinda like the sound of Roxanne Matthews," he says again with his sexy smirk and teasing wink. I kind of like—really like actually—the sound of Roxanne Matthews as well, but I'm not going to confess that to Chad, because as usual he's just teasing and trying to get a rise out of me. And Roxanne Matthews—Donaghey—does not bite when Chad tells her to.

"Not funny, you dick," I jeer, playfully slapping his abs again.

"Sorry Rox," he says softly, getting up, and pulling off his hoodie. Underneath he has on a tight white Nike shirt and I stifle a laugh looking at him in that; it makes me think of dirty thoughts—Nike slogan wise—that I want to with Chad.

"You might want this. You chundered all over that pretty red dress you had on," he tells me, breaking my dirty thoughts.

"Oh, I don't want to take your jumper though," I reply with a smile.

Still my Girl

He chuckles, a deep sexy chuckle that makes his abs vibrate and he teases me, "Well, I'm all for you going home in your birthday suit Rox. But it's freezing outside."

"Fine. But no looking," I retort when the doctor comes back in.

He makes quick work of disconnecting all the wires attached to my body and I get up off the bed—turning my back to Chad—and letting the hospital gown fall down my arms to the floor.

I feel incredibly exposed and turn back to look at Chad who doesn't have his eyes closed but is staring at me like he actually likes what he's seeing.

I slip his jumper on—pulling it over my head—and I'm shocked that it only just grazes the top of my thighs, which makes me self conscious but it's better than walking out of the hospital in a g-string and bralette.

The doctor explains my discharge to me, telling me about the painkillers I can take and he tells me to take it easy and rest for the day.

I nod, thanking him and pull down the down jumper a little —taking Chad's hand—and the prescription from the doctor.

I shove it in the pocket at the front of the jumper and follow Chad out.

Walking out of the hospital he asks, "So what do you wanna do for the arvo?"

"Watch a movie and eat an entire tub of Connoisseur Vanilla Caramel Brownie ice cream."

"Oh fuck yeah," Chad curses. "That stuff is ripper. We'll pick some up on the way home."

"Awesome," I reply eagerly.

I could get used to this, the caring side of Chad coming out again. It makes my heart hammer in my chest, because even though I pushed my feelings aside—told myself I can't love him—I absolutely still do love him, even more than before.

15. *Chad*

Driving home I can't help but stare at Rox out of the corner of my eyes. Seeing her in my hoodie—with her legs crossed underneath her—on the seat of my car is such a fucking turn on.

It practically shows her pussy, which is only covered by a g-string.

I'd had to tell my dick to calm the fuck down when I sneakily checked her out whilst she put the hoodie on before we left the hospital. I'd honestly forgotten—ok, not forgotten—but hadn't pictured her arse looking so fucking delectable in my thoughts of her.

I'm practically gunning it home, after our quick stop at the supermarket to grab her ice cream and some other snacks. It feels just like old times—except for her wearing my hoodie—when we'd sit in the rumpus room together watching Disney movies.

She'd sit between my legs, and I'd play with her hair and as I'd gotten older I'd had to restrain myself to not crack a fat, especially when I'd massage her shoulders and she'd moan. I can still hear that sound in my head, and I'm hoping to hear it in person again.

Once home she runs to the bathroom, whilst I put the chicken chips in a bowl and grab a soup spoon to eat the ice cream straight from the tub.

I flop down on the couch, nearly creaming my daks when she comes out—still in my hoodie and nothing else—after having brushed her hair out. It falls across her shoulders, and she looks absolutely stunning.

My mind is wandering to all kind of dirty—delicious—thoughts, like pulling her onto my lap and kissing her zealously.

She sits down next to me, again folding her legs underneath her body.

"So Rox, what're watching?"

"Anything, maybe a mystery."

I flick through Netflix, deciding on a thriller.

I hand Rox the tub of Connoisseur ice cream, and she opens it, digging the spoon in and putting it into her mouth, moaning as she savours the sweet vanilla flavour.

I'm seriously about to crack a fat.

After about fifteen minutes—once she's consumed half the ice cream—she shifts back a little , and moves to sit between my legs. I absentmindedly start running my hands through her hair, massaging her head gently, and she sighs, moans and before I know it she's asleep, her back against my chest.

I'm having a hard time focusing on the movie, instead, I'm staring down at her, feeling like the luckiest son of a bitch ever to have her in my arms.

But I want so much more from her.

The movie is pretty fucking lame—what I watched of it—and when the credits are rolling Rox yawns and wakes up, looking up at me smiling.

"Did I miss the ending?" she asks softly.

"Yeah, they all died," I reply chuckling.

She turns her head a little, so our eyes meet and she raises an eyebrow at me, asking, "Really? That's crap."

Again I chuckle, playfully poking her in the belly.

"I'm kidding Rox."

"Mmm, yeah. Um..." she mutters, biting down on her lip, and looking towards her lap and then back at me.

"What?" I ask, raising my eyebrow, and giving her a smirk.

"Something's poking me in the back," she declares, her lips curving up at the corner of her mouth.

"Yeah, what's that?" I taunt, knowing it's my hard as fuck dick from having her arse pressed against it for an hour whilst she slept.

"It's...um, long and hard," she says with a cheeky laugh.

I laugh, loudly, taunting her with a smirk, "Long and hard, huh?"

"Yeah, it's probably the remote," she says moving off my lap. I miss the contact of her body against mine straight away but laugh when she shrieks, "Oh my god, Chad. Your dick is hard!"

"Yeah, well, you were rubbing your sweet arse all over me in your sleep, Rox."

She playfully punches me in the abs.

"Oh no, you didn't Rox," I jeer tickling her and pulling her onto my lap. She's looking at me doe-eyed, trying not to smile and break into a fit of giggles.

My dick is screaming at me—to take things further—so I do, brazenly pulling her down against my chest, our lips just a centimetre apart.

She takes a deep breath in, about to say my name when she exhales softly, but I don't let her say a word, instead, I kiss her, hard, zealously and the sweet moan she makes deepening the kiss makes my heart pound.

Fuck, she knows how to kiss.

16. Roxanne

Still kissing Chad, I moan against his lips, grinding against his impressive erection. Even with the fabric between us, I feel like I'm going to come.

My mind can't focus on anything but how amazing pashing Chad is. It's like I've never been kissed—never done anything sexual—until this very moment.

Breathless, I break the kiss, flipping my hair back and pushing it behind me.

Chad moans, smirking at me, showing his gorgeous double dimple. That look that never fails to make my stomach flip flop.

"You look sexy in my hoodie, Rox," he says, his voice husky and so sexy it makes my body throb.

I want him so much, but I'm nervous.

"Don't say that."

Chad chuckles softly. "It's true Rox," he tells me with a smirk, grabbing my hips—the hem of the hoodie—when he continues. "But you know what?"

"What?" I ask, biting down on my lip worriedly.

"You'd look even sexier out of it."

I playfully smack his abs, jeering, "Chad, stop."

"I want you Rox," he declares, the smirk suddenly absent from his face.

I don't know if that means he's being sincere or just playing me to get sex.

"Um....I....I," I stammer, again biting my lip.

I'm giving away all my tells. He'll see right through me.

"Admit it Rox...you want me to," he says, gathering the hoodie more and lifting it up a little to expose my stomach. He takes his lip between his teeth then, moaning as he glares at me when I sigh and sit up in his lap, pulling the hoodie off over my head. I throw it on the floor, and Chad looks at me with lust flaring in his eyes.

"God, you're stunning, Rox," he purrs, grabbing my waist and pulling me down for a fierce kiss.

Being more exposed to him—in my underwear—is making me feel so wet. He turns me on so much.

Whilst kissing me, his arms wrap around my back and he undoes my bra like a pro.

I try not to think about how many times he's done that before. It falls down my arms between us when he pulls back from the kiss. His eyes wander my body again like he's admiring me. And for some reason, I know this is going to be it.

I'm going to lose my virginity to Chad tonight.

Still my Girl

"Do you know how fucking beautiful you are Rox?" He asks, rhetorically.

Leaning closer to him a little I giggle, and taunt him, "You're fucking gorgeous Chad."

"Ooo, Rox swore," he says chuckling again.

Laughing myself, I press my hands against his chest and can feel his skin heat with my touch even with his t-shirt on.

With my lips just a breath away from his, I whisper, "Do I turn you on, Chad?"

He pushes me back a little. "You're kidding, right? My dick is hard as for you Rox."

I moan, rocking my pelvis over his erection and he groans, loudly, cursing, "Fuck Rox."

Again I giggle, loving making him moan and I slide down his legs a little, yanking his trackies down.

He's commando and his hard dick springs forward.

My eyes boggle seeing his glorious, hard dick again. His dick that is hard for me.

Stroking it softly in my fists he murmurs, closing his eyes for a moment before he groans and says through his gritted teeth, "Mmm Rox, your hands on me baby. So good."

I laugh, leaning down towards his dick. "Yeah, how about this?" I query pushing my hands up under his t-shirt and taking his hard dick into my mouth, completely.

17. Chad

Oh, fuck me! Rox is...fuck! Sucking my dick...

Yanking my trackies down my legs more, Rox pulls back at little, taking my dick out of her mouth slowly.
Licking the slit with teasing strokes of her tongue, she moans an appreciative 'mmm' and I throb inside her mouth.
It's absolutely fucking amazing watching her bob and up and down on my rock hard length. No bj has ever felt this good.
She's making sucking sounds, her hands gripping the base of my dick and my balls, squeezing hard.
"God fuck, Rox!" I call out with a moan. "Fuck, suck me baby."
She continues bobbing up and down on my dick, taking it in all the way and out again, licking the length and the tip every time like it's a delicious lollipop.
And oh fuck me dead, its fucking ecstasy. If I don't stop her now, I'm going to come down her throat and I'm so fucking

Still my Girl

hard right now—so hard for her—that I want to slam my cock into her pussy.

Grabbing her hair, I pull her off my dick.

"Rox, that feels damn good, baby. But I want to fuck you."

She whimpers, but a smile turns the corner of her lips up.

I pull off my t-shirt and grab Rox around the waist picking her up into my arms.

Standing up from the couch she wraps her legs around my arse, and her arms around my neck, crushing her lips to mine in a kiss that makes my whole body throb.

Whilst carrying her to her bedroom, we continue kissing fiercely.

Reaching her bed, I put her down—breaking the kiss—standing up to admire her sexy body.

"God, Rox. You're stunning baby."

"Back at you Chad," she replies, sitting up and pulling me down against her body.

She kisses me, and it's such a fucking turn on.

Murmuring against my lips she pulls back a little, whispering, "Touch me Chad."

"Oh, Rox, I'm gonna do so much more than touch you."

She blushes crimson, biting down on her lip, whispering softly, "A first."

Those two simple words make me groan.

So absolutely fucking sexy.

And exciting.

Caz May

I'm the only guy to taste her sweet pussy and I honestly can't wait another second.

Dropping to my knees I grip her hips, bringing her arse to the edge of the bed.

She's looking down at me, and giving her a smirk I lick her pussy without warning. She moans, a delicious loud, dirty moan that makes her whole body twitch.

"Mmm, Rox," I taunt, biting her clit, and pushing two fingers into her pussy.

She's so wet, so ready, but I want more from her.

I want to make her come—from this—and also from my cock buried inside her.

Teasingly I kiss her clit, sucking it in between my lips, and she writhes beneath me.

Her pussy is tight against my fingers, making me wonder for a moment if she's a virgin.

Slowly I withdraw my fingers, and replace them with my tongue, lapping up her arousal with my tongue in teasing circles.

"Oh my god, Chad...that...that feels...fuck!"

I love that getting her pussy licked is making her swear. It's so deliciously dirty.

Again I kiss her bud, my lips open and pressed against her skin whilst I flick my tongue against her.

She grips the sheets in her fists, her whole body twitching, shaking as she rides the wave of her orgasm, coming all over my face.

Still my Girl

She's breathless and panting when I lie over her body, smiling at her and brushing her hair away from her face.

"You taste delicious, Rox."

"Really?"

"Yeah, baby. Wanna taste?"

She nods, giggling and I kiss her.

She moans loudly, licking my lips and playing with my tongue teasingly. It's making my cock scream.

I need to fuck her.

Breaking the kiss, I lie back on the bed, and murmur in her ear, "Rox, I want to fuck you, baby."

"Mmm, I'm um...on the pill," she tells me softly.

Music to my fucking ears.

I'm going to fuck her bare, and I almost come just thinking about that.

"Fuck Rox, I want you so bad. Are you sure you want me?"

She laughs at me, rolling over so she's facing me.

Her hair falls over her shoulders and brushing it back, my eyes scan her body, her fucking glorious naked body.

Softly I kiss her, pulling her body against mine with a hand on her hips.

My rock hard dick is at her entrance, and I sway my crotch against hers, coating the tip of my dick in her arousal.

I break the kiss, teasing her, "Your pussy is wet as fuck for me baby. Tell me you want my dick inside you, Rox."

"Fuck me please, Chad," she murmurs, biting down on her lip and staring right into my eyes.

I feel that look right in the fucking feels, all through my body that is on fire with desire.

I never in a million fucking years thought I'd ever kiss her again, let alone be about to slide inside her sweet pussy and fuck her until she screams my name.

Crashing my lips to hers in a heated kiss, I slam my pelvis against hers, shoving my dick hard into her pussy.

She whimpers against my lips as though it hurts, and slowly thrusting in and out, I break the kiss, and ask her softly, "You ok, Rox? Please tell me if I'm hurting you."

"I'm ok, please...please, just fuck me harder," she says a little breathlessly, again biting down on her lip.

I thrust a little harder, feeling her body start to relax whilst her pussy clenches around my dick inside her.

Her sweet pussy that is tight—as a vice—gripping me, and sending me closer to the edge.

This hot spooning missionary sex is fucking euphoric and looking at Rox again when she pushes her pelvis against mine, starting to moan I question her, "You good, baby?"

"Yep, fuck, better than good. Amazing."

"Mmm, fuck Rox," I moan, pumping my dick in and out of her body harder. "You gonna come, baby?"

"Yes, oh god Chad, yes," she nearly screams out.

Still my Girl

She's so close to coming, so grabbing her around the waist
I pull her on top of me.

"Ride me Rox. Come on my dick, baby."

She lays over me, kissing me hard and fiercely, whilst
bouncing her pussy on my dick.

And it's absolute bliss.

Breaking the kiss she sits up, holding her hands above her
head whilst she continues impaling herself on my length,
up, down, on it and off before she takes me completely
inside her again, screaming out, "Oh fuck! Chad! Fuck!"

I feel her whole body trembling, her pussy clenching, and
milking my dick.

"That's it Rox, come for me baby. Come for me."

"Fuck, fuck, fuck!" she screams out again, collapsing
against my chest, shivering from the wave of her release
when I lose myself inside her, filling her tight pussy with a
shitload of my hot cum.

Taking a deep breath, I softly kiss her, whispering against
her lips, "Damn, Rox, baby, that was incredible."

She doesn't reply, just murmurs softly, and kisses me again.

I've fucked plenty of chicks but never has it felt that
fucking amazing.

Absolutely fucking incredible, fucking life-changing.

I want to tell her how I feel about her, but the words are
caught in my throat, and when she breaks the kiss and lays
down beside me I pull her against my side.

Kissing her forehead, I ask softly, "You good baby?"

Caz May

"Yeah, Chad. Thank you for another first."

I reply, "No worries," giving her a sweet quick kiss and closing my eyes.

She's already drifting off to sleep, and holding her close as I fall asleep I ponder that statement.

Another first.

I wonder for a moment if it was the first time she'd gone cowgirl or if it was her actual first time.

And I feel like I've been punched in the guts when she shifts to be closer to me because I should've known by how tight she was that she was a virgin.

I fucked her so hard, and it was her first time.

I'm such an arsehole.

But damn, she saved her first time for me, and fuck me does that make me love her—my sweet Roxanne—more than ever.

18. *Chad*

Sometime in the middle of the night, I carefully climb out of Rox's bed, untangling myself from her arms that she's wrapped around me whilst sleeping.

I feel like such an arsehole—for skipping out on her—and taking her virginity, so hard and rough.

I should have taken it slow, shown her that I'm in love with her and not just after a quick fuck.

That's the absolute last thing I want from Rox, but here I am creeping out of her bedroom—starkers—like she's a one night stand.

I stop at her bedroom door, staring at her like a damn lunatic, watching her exposed breasts rise and fall with her breathing. And I'm cracking a fat from knowing how good —how fucking incredible—it felt to be inside her pussy and wrapped around her sexy as fuck body.

I'm so fucked—absolutely pussy whipped—for her, Roxanne Genevieve Donaghey.

And I can't be with her.

I have to let go—kick my feelings to the curb again.

Caz May

She might be living with me, but I'm damn sure she's neglected to mention that fact to her brother and I'm not going to face him again. He'll probably break every bone in my body if he finds out I fucked Rox.

Back in my room, I crawl into bed, closing my eyes and thinking about Rox in the next room.
Every cell in my damn body wants to go back into her bedroom, to wake up in her arms and have hot as hell morning sex with her—but I can't.
She's not my girl.
She cant be my girl, even if I want her to be.
Ever since I was a kid I've fought my feelings for her, pushing them aside because falling for your best friend's little sister is wrong—so wrong because she's like a little sister to me.

Who am I fucking kidding? Rox, my sister?

That thought is absolutely fucking laughable.
I've never seen her as a little sister, and now I've had her completely she's mine, my girl.
I drift to sleep thinking of her—of the best sex of my life—wondering if she could really be my girl, or if I'm only dreaming.

Still my Girl

Maybe she doesn't feel anything for me and was just using me to lose her virginity. Seems unlikely, but falling for your best friends little sister is just as unlikely.

Grabbing a muesli bar for breakfast I skip out before Rox gets up.
Eating it I whizz in and out of the morning traffic, going to grab a cappuccino before I head to the bar early.

It's just gone ten, so there's plenty of time to tidy up and check the stock levels for the lunch hour rush.
Reaching up to get the new Jack Daniels bottle from the top shelf behind the bar I feel someone step up behind me. The bitch that kissed me a few months ago is in my personal space, about to jump me.

Turning around I push her away a little but she stumbles into me and tries to lay a kiss on me again.
Turning my head to the side her lips meet my cheek and I slide down the length of the bar to get away from her.
She's fuming at me, scowling. "What's with you?" she snaps, glaring at me when I don't reply.
"Do you have a girlfriend?"
"No, but I'm in love with someone," I tell her, thoughts of Rox filling my mind.

"Right, well, whatever, Chad," she snaps at me walking out from behind the bar.

I potter around the bar then, cleaning and serving the old drunk guys that always come in.

Rox is on my mind all damn day, and I practically have a stiffy all day from thinking about her.

Part of me wants to rush home, tell her I'm head over heels in love with her—fuck her into tomorrow—and make love to her until dusk the next day.

But I also know that I can't.

I can't be the guy for her.

❤

I end up doing a double shift because kissing bitch decided to up and leave, instead of working her shift.

And in some way, I'm happy about it, as it makes it easier to avoid Rox, to not have to see her and face my feelings head-on.

By the time I clean up the bar and leave it's pitch black outside and the streets are quiet.

I get home in record time, creep into the house and pass Rox's room to find she's asleep. Her door is ajar, and I watch her for a moment—feeling like a creeper—getting a mega hard on from staring at her.

It's funny how before actually physically being with her I never had this reaction to her, but after being with her and

Still my Girl

giving in to the lust for her pulsing through my body I only have to think of her for my body to react.

I think I always pushed the attraction I had for her away, because I told myself I shouldn't feel it—not for her—but I just can't help it now, knowing how amazing it is to kiss her, and be inside her sweet pussy.

God, I'm so fucking hard right now.

I feel like sneaking into her bedroom and climbing in beside her, so she wakes up in my arms.

But she probably hates me for skipping out on her last night, so I instead head into the bathroom, stripping out of my work clothes that reek of alcohol.

Turning on the taps, I wait for the bathroom to fill with steam and yank my boxers to the floor over my stiffy.

Stepping into the shower, I slide the glass screen closed and stand under the spray of water, closing my eyes and running my hands through my hair to slick it back. The hot water feels divine against my skin.

And grabbing my body wash, I squeeze a dollop into my palm—lathering it all over my body—grabbing my hard as fuck dick in a fist. Leaning back against the shower wall I close my eyes, stroking my dick slowly and picturing Rox riding me.

I can't help the moans that are escaping my lips, my breath coming out as panting.

Cupping my balls in my other hand I squeeze them, still pumping my hand up and down my hard length.

It's barely a minute before I'm screaming out her name— cum shooting out of my dick in a rush—and coating the shower screen.

Rox wasn't even in the shower and I came harder than I ever have from wanking thinking about her.

After quickly washing up and wiping the face washer over the shower screen, I turn off the taps before getting out and wrapping a fluffy towel around my waist.

Heading to my bedroom, I sneak a peek into Rox's room; thankfully she's still asleep. Closing the door behind me I whisper, *'I love you Rox'* and I head to bed thinking of whether I'm ready for her to hear those words, and even if I should tell her at all.

19. Roxanne

A couple of days after losing my v-card to Chad, I wake up with a start, whacking my arm against my alarm clock by my bed.

But the blaring sound doesn't stop, and I grunt, pulling my pillow over my head in frustration. It's obviously Chad's alarm that's blaring, but he doesn't appear to be getting up or turning it off.

I don't really want to face him, since he's been avoiding me since we slept together. My heart hurts that even after having sex with him, he still pushed me away like I mean nothing to him.

He runs hot and cold, wanting me one minute—one day— and then completely ignoring me the next minute—next day.

His alarm is still blaring, so getting out of bed—putting on my sheep slippers—I head down the hallway to his room. The door is slightly ajar, and I knock softly, but he doesn't answer.

Caz May

Tentatively I open the door, entering his room to find him in bed, asleep—despite the blaring alarm—dead to the world.

Stepping up to his bedside I slap his alarm off and softly shake him to wake him up. He lets out a rather loud moan, rolling over and grabbing my arm, pulling me down to the bed.

His grip is tight and I fall against him. He moans again, pulling me into his side. And I grunt my annoyance.

"Chad, seriously, wake up!"

"Huh, what? Fuck!" He curses, his eyes fluttering open.

He shifts back from me and looks at me shocked.

"Shit, Rox, what're you doing in my bed?"

"Your alarm was screaming, so I came in to turn it off and you pulled me into bed with you."

"Sorry, about both of those."

"Whatever," I spit at him, standing up. "You can go back to sleep now."

He grabs my hand.

"Rox, you ok?"

I turn to look at him—feeling my heart shatter in my chest —completely mesmerised by his blue eyes that make me melt.

"No, Chad, I'm not ok. I'm really hurt."

He gulps, pulling my arm so I again fall onto the bed.

"I'm sorry, Rox."

Still my Girl

"Stop! You're not sorry. You got what you wanted and now you're just ignoring me like it never happened, just like you did after we first kissed. But this is worse and I..."

I stop talking, again trying to stand up but he wraps his arm around my waist.

I'm fighting back tears, sniffing when I tell him, "I'm going to move out."

"Come on Rox. You don't need to do that. I said I'm sorry."

"That's just it, Chad. You shouldn't have to anything to be sorry about but it's obvious you don't feel the same about me as I do for you. And I can't stay here anymore."

He chuckles softly—smirking—making my stomach flip flop.

"And how do you feel about me Rox?"he taunts, with his sexy smirk on his face.

I laugh then, trying to calm my breathing and pounding heart.

"I'm in love with you, Chad," I confess.

He gulps—swallowing hard—about to say something when I blurt out, "And when we slept together it was my first time."

"I know Rox, and I'm so fucking sorry for pushing you away. I honestly thought I'd hurt you so bad, and that you'd hate me for taking away your virginity like I didn't fucking give a shit at all."

"You didn't hurt me that night. It was amazing, and I'm so glad I waited for you, but you ignoring me after that hurt so bad Chad."

"I'm sorry, Rox. I really am. Sleeping with you was incredible. I felt something that night I've never felt before but I was too afraid to feel that way about you."

"Why? Don't you care about me at all?"

"Of course I fucking care about you Rox. I'm so fucking in love with you it hurts every second I can't be with you."

My heart leaps in my chest, my mind racing whilst I process his confession.

"Then why push me away?"

"Because even though I'm not talking to Jessie if he found out he'd kill me."

"True," I agree laughing, and smiling at him when he pulls me down to lie next to him.

"So, Roxanne Genevieve Donaghey, how do you feel about me again?"

I look at him—dead in the eyes—and smile wider, before kissing him, and whispering against his delectable lips, "I love you Chad Tristan Matthews."

He breaks the kiss, a sweeter than sugar smile on his face.

"I love you to, Rox."

Again I kiss him—hard and dirty—making my whole body throb with want for him. I don't want to leave, but I have to.

20. *Chad*

After confessing my feelings to Rox, and having her confess she feels the same she kisses me, hard and dirty.

But breaking the kiss a few minutes later—breathless—I feel her pull away, her legs slipping over the edge of the bed.

"Rox, baby, where do you think you're going?"

"I told you I'm moving out."

"Aww, come on Rox, please. Just stay with me."

"Why Chad? Just because we feel the same way about each other doesn't mean living together is the right thing."

"Of course it's the right thing. I'm in love with you Rox. I wanna be with you, all the fucking time. Have you fall asleep in my arms every night and wake up to kiss you good morning."

She's standing by the bed now, looking down at me.

"Fine," she replies with a huff. "But it has to just be me, Chad. No other girls."

"Scouts honour, baby," I tease, sitting up, and grabbing her by the waist to pull her back down onto the bed for yet

Caz May

another kiss. I can't get enough of her, and I doubt I ever
will.

Breaking the kiss—with her still on top of me—I brush her
hair back from her cheeks and smirk at her.
"So Roxanne," I taunt. "How about we go on a date?"
She laughs—sweetly—smiling at me.
"A date huh? Where would we go on this date?"
I sit up, making her sit up and straddle me, her pussy
aligned with my rock hard morning wood.
I kiss her, rocking my dick against her pussy that's barely
covered by her lacy knickers.
Against her lips, I whisper, "To the beach."
She breaks the kiss, moaning from my dick teasing her.
"Why the beach?"
"So I can ogle your sexy body in a skimpy bikini," I tease,
giving her a smirk and kissing her hard before she can
reply.
"Oh is that so?" Rox taunts me, laughing sweetly. "Will you
be wearing budgie smugglers?"
"Not a chance in hell, Rox," I reply, laughing, and letting out
a moan when she rocks her pussy over my dick again.
I pull her down for a kiss, reaching down between our
bodies to rub her clit through the lace of her knickers.
She moans against my lips, pulling back and asking, "Are
you trying to get into my knickers, Chad?"

Still my Girl

"Oh, you bet I am, Roxanne," I taunt, pushing the lace aside.

Laughing, I tease her, "Damn, Rox, you're wet, baby."

She playfully slaps my chest. "Stop, Chad," she protests.

"Only if you rub your sweet pussy on my dick."

She gasps—when I flick her clit again—rubbing my thumb pad over the sensitive spot. She doesn't say anything but starts sliding over my dick, teasing me by not letting it slip inside.

And it feels damn good.

"Damn, Rox, baby, that feels so good."

She moans, loudly, still gliding over my dick, from my balls all the way to the tip. "Chad, I'm going to come."

"Oh yeah, Rox, baby. Me to. Keep going."

Again she slides her body—her pussy—over my dick, and in a rush, I explode, ropes of cum spurting out all over my stomach.

I feel Rox tremble with her release, and she moans, letting out a soft 'fuck'. Leaning over me, she kisses me sweetly.

I pull back, whispering to her, "Damn Rox. That was hot."

She's looking down at me, smiling at me, softly saying, "Another first."

"I love that you saved all your firsts for me, Rox."

"Me, too," she says excitedly, jumping up off the bed.

"Where do you think you're going?"

"To get ready for the beach. Gotta find my other bikini."

"I'm excited just thinking about it," I reply laughing.

Caz May

I want to pull her back down for a kiss, but she's right that we need to get ready for the beach trip. She sashays out of my room, wiggling her hips seductively and I climb out of bed, heading to the bathroom to clean up and get ready myself.

The beach is relatively quiet for a warm arvo, but I'm kinda glad of that fact because Rox looks absolutely sexy as sin in a blue and white tie-dye bikini.

The top accentuates her perfect tits, her cleavage on full display. And the bottoms have ties at the side—sitting on her hips—and just above the top of her arse.

What makes the bikini even more sexy—for my eyes only —is the fact that I know what her body looks like underneath the barely there fabric.

Being with her at the beach is such a turn on, and thankfully being in the water no one can see my hard on. Playing in the water she splashes me, giggling.

"Oh, it's like that is it?" I taunt her, grabbing her around the waist.

"Yep," she replies with a laugh before squirming out of my arms and swimming away, before splashing me again.

"Oh no, you didn't Rox," I taunt her again, diving under the water and scooping her up in my arms.

She protests, squirming in my arms. I squeeze her arse, chuckling before I throw her in playfully.

Still my Girl

When she surfaces, she's smiling, and rushes towards me, kissing me fiercely. Her hands find my dick and through the fabric of my boardies, she strokes my length.

"Seems like I turn you on?"

"You'd turn any guy on in that sexy bikini, Rox."

She giggles, her hand slipping inside the boardies to continue touching me.

I slip a finger inside her bikini bottoms, inside her pussy and again I take her mouth in a kiss.

We keep kissing and teasing each other for a few minutes, so close to again falling over the edge when I pull back.

"Rox, baby. We need to stop."

"Why?"

"We're in public."

"Fine," Rox replies defiantly, winking at me, squeezing my dick before pulling her hand out.

"It's just like old times though, being at the beach with you."

Rox laughs, tipping her head back. "Oh yeah totally, except for the kissing and touching."

"Yeah," I reply, leaning into her ear to whisper, "and the dirty sex we're going to have when I get you back home."

"Oh really? What makes you think I'm going to have sex with you again, huh?" she taunts me, smirking.

"You love me Rox. And I'm irresistible."

"Nah, you...irresistible, pfft."

She's still smirking when she walks out of the surf.

And I watch her for a moment before running after her and grabbing her around the waist from behind.

"Just you wait, Roxanne," I taunt, whispering in her ear. She shivers, from my breath against her sensitive skin. She frees herself from my grip—gazing back at me—and she gives me a sexy smirk before running across the beach to her jeep.

Running I follow her, thinking about stripping her of the bikini and following through on the dirty sex I'd promised her.

21. Chad

The moment we get home from the beach—the very minute—we step inside the front door Rox is kissing me. She's taking control, and my already hard dick is screaming in my boardies.

Still kissing her, I hook my fingers into the side of her bikini bottoms to touch her pussy. She whimpers against my lips, pulling back from the kiss, and locking her eyes on mine with a smirk on her face.

Starting to walk backwards towards the bathroom, her eyes don't leave mine. I follow her—wanting to run at her—but instead I take tentative steps, telling myself to take it slow.

Reaching the bathroom I find her standing against the shower screen, twirling her tie-dye bikini top on her finger, again with the seductive smirk on her gorgeous face.

Seeing her half-naked—teasing me—is making my practically already rock hard dick throb in my boardies.

"Damn Rox. You're such a tease," I taunt her, stepping closer and grabbing her around the waist.

"Me? A tease?" she says, shaking her head, and fiddling with the ties of her bikini bottoms.

I can't tear my eyes from her, watching as her fingers undo the knots and the fabric drops to the floor.

I yank my boardies down, still feasting on Rox starkers in front of me. She's beaming, and she's honestly never looked so fucking breathtaking, so sexy.

She slides the shower screen across, stepping under the warm spray of water, beckoning me with a finger. I prowl into the shower—sliding the screen across—like a damn tiger, eager for his prey.

Grabbing Rox around the waist, I growl, "You're mine, Roxanne."

She murmurs, pressing her body into mine, and kissing me fiercely, like a damn animal. It's such a carnal, animalistic kiss; a kiss that is making my whole pulse with lust for my sexy Roxanne.

Moaning she breaks the kiss, stepping back from me to grab a bar of soap. Locking her eyes on mine again, she smirks and starts rubbing it all over her body; into a white creamy lather. I literally can't stop staring, my dick is practically pulsating, jumping up and down, so eager to have her; be inside her.

"Mmm, Rox. You look so sexy doing that," I tell her with a groan, biting down on my lip.

"Wanna help? Or I could do you?" she asks, with innocent flirtation in her tone.

Still my Girl

"Oh, you're so doing me, baby," I tease, wrenching the soap from her hand and dropping it the floor. She makes a shrieking sound, about to open her mouth to protest, but I silence her with a zealous kiss. My lips still on hers, deepening the kiss with my tongue dancing over her lips I back her against the tiles. She breaks the kiss, panting, and looks up at me all doe-eyed, her lips red and swollen from my kiss.

"Fuck me, Chad," she purrs, making my dick throb.

Gripping her waist I turn our bodies around so my back is against the tiles, and I pull her back against me, slamming my dick inside her pussy without warning. My knees are bent, and she's practically sitting on my lap, riding my dick. I fist her hair, tugging on it to bring her face closer to mine for a kiss, that is frantic and all tongues dancing together whilst I thrust into her pussy.

I've had sex in the shower before, but this, fuck, it's never been this intense.

Hearing Rox moan, I'm so close to exploding inside her, so I whisper in her ear, "Come for me Rox, baby, come on my dick."

She impales herself down harder on my dick, it hitting the sweet spot inside her that makes her curse and I reach down to rub a finger over her clit; making her whole body spasm in a hard sudden release, a shaking orgasm that even with the warm water cascading over us she's shivering.

Getting off my dick—before I shoot my load into her—she turns around and kisses me softly.

"Fuck, Chad. That was amazing."

"You bet it was, baby," I reply, kissing her cheek and stepping aside to turn off the taps.

She's grinning, following me naked to my bedroom after we leave the shower. Falling against the bed I pull her down for a kiss. My dick is still painfully hard, and I want her again; this time also wanting to fill her with my hot cum, until it's dripping out of her pussy.

Breaking the kiss, I trail kisses over her body, over every inch of her skin, taking my time to kiss and lick her scar. She squirms a little then, as though she's uncomfortable with the gesture.

I look up at her, smiling. "Your body is so fucking glorious, Rox. So damn sexy, and mine, baby."

She giggles softly, giving me a smile before I dive between her legs to kiss and lick her clit and pussy like it's my last damn meal. Delving my tongue inside her makes her buck her hips against my face, and it makes my dick pulse between my legs.

She's close to the falling over the edge again, and I'm about to come myself, so I stretch over her body again, kissing her furiously. She cups my cheeks, deepening the kiss and tasting herself on my lips.

Still my Girl

My dick is teasing her entrance and pulling back from the kiss, I brush her hair back from her face. "Do you trust me Rox?"

"Of course, Chad," she murmurs.

"Good," I reply, a slight smirk on my face. Standing up I look down at her, grabbing her legs, and sliding her down so her arse is on the very edge of the bed.

"Spread you legs for me, baby," I instruct her. She quickly obeys, and I step in between them, slamming my dick inside her, in and out furiously making her moan.

Grabbing her thighs I demand, "Put your legs over my shoulders Rox."

Agin she obeys, biting down on her lip with anticipation. I thrust into her hard, driving my dick all the way inside her pussy, my body baring down over her legs.

"Oh my god, Chad! Fuck!" She moans, her pussy swallowing my dick so I'm balls deep inside her. It feels absolutely fucking incredible, even more so when she starts to clench around me, her pussy spasming as she heads towards release.

I pull out, nearly all the way, so only the tip of my dick is inside her and I softly say, "Tell me what you want Rox."

Her eyes lock on mine when she pants, "For you to fuck me hard, Chad. Make me come on your cock."

Hearing her say cock instead of dick is really erotic, a mega turn on and it makes my cock throb when I slam back inside her, thrusting deep and hard. She's moaning, and panting, meeting my thrusts with her hips.

And when she screams out, "Oh fuck! I'm coming!" Her release is hard, her whole body trembling, milking my sudden climax deep inside her.

"Fuck, Rox. That was fucking incredible baby," I tell her pulling out and stepping back from the edge of the bed.

She puts her legs down and scoots back to lay in the middle of the bed. I lay down beside her and kiss her softly.

"Rox, you ok?"

"Yeah, better than ok. That was really amazing. I've never come so hard in my life."

"Another first?"

"Yeah, all the firsts for you, Chad," she says with a smile, kissing me sweetly. "I love you, Chad."

"I love you too, Roxanne. I always have. You're my girl."

She smiles at my words, again kissing me with so much love and I pull her into my arms. I don't want to be anywhere else.

22. Roxanne

After the most amazing sex ever, Chad pulls me into his arms, kissing me. Every time he kisses me, I feel like melting, as though I could self combust. Being with him is so much better than I ever imagined it could be.

We're still lying naked in his bed, our legs entangled and his arms around my waist. He's smiling at me and I laugh, feeling suddenly self-conscious.

"What's up baby?" he asks.

"I was just thinking about Jessie."

He chuckles, deep, putting a hand to his heart. "Why are you thinking about your brother after we just fucked?

"I don't know. I guess I just feel guilty."

"Yeah, I get you. But you're a grown woman Rox. You don't have to tell him anything."

"I know, but I feel like I should, especially now."

"Yeah, why is that?"

I scoot closer to him, hoping that he won't get angry at me for what I'm about to say. Softly I tell him, "Jessie's getting married to Teagan in a couple of months."

"Yeah, sucks for him."

"Maybe you should make amends with him."

"I don't know if I can Rox. Especially because he's still marrying her after what she did."

"Was it all her fault though?"

He playfully grabs my side, taunting me, "Hey, whose side are you on?"

"Yours, I just want my brother to be happy. And you too."

"I know Rox. But she kissed me. I did kinda want her, but I never made a move. I wouldn't do that."

"I know that. And I think deep down Jess does too, but he loves Teagan and it was easier to push you away, given your history."

"Yeah, I'm not proud of the old me Rox. But honestly, I only behaved that way because I thought I couldn't have you."

"I've always wanted you Chad."

"I know. And I'm sorry for taking so long to own up to my feelings for you. Once we kissed after the karaoke it was only you I wanted Rox."

"Yeah, so will you make amends with Jessie? For me?" I ask, giving him my best puppy dog eyed pout.

"Fine, but only because you're asking me to," He agrees, with a nod. "And because you look so damn cute and sexy right now."

Still my Girl

We both laugh, and he kisses me hard and passionately taking my breath away. Being with him has only made me love him more, but I'm worried my older brother isn't going to like the fact I'm with Chad. I'm scared for his reaction, but I don't want to hide anything from him. Pulling back from Chad's kiss, I smile at him before closing my eyes.

"You tired, baby?" he asks me, kissing my forehead softly, his lips brushing my hairline.

"Yeah," I groan.

"Must have been the multiple orgasms you had," he jeers, pulling the sheet up over us. The word orgasms sounds so illicit coming from his lips; I want to hear it again.

"What did you say?" I murmur.

"Orgasms, Rox. I gave you multiple orgasms," he says enunciating the words into multiple syllables.

"Mmm," I murmur, turning in his embrace and kissing him, still with my eyes closed.

He laughs against my lips before pulling back.

"Goodnight, Roxanne, my girl."

"Goodnight, Chad," I reply, smiling from hearing him call me his girl.

I couldn't be happier, but as I drift to sleep I wonder if that happiness is going to be short-lived when Jessie finds out.

23. Roxanne

I feel guilty. Guilty that I'm about to call my older brother, to trick him into a double date.

Sitting on my bed, I'm clutching my phone in my hand, looking up at Chad standing in front of me. He's smirking at me, which isn't helping my nerves.

I've barely spoken to Jessie since he kicked me out and he thinks I'm living with Nellie. I don't know why he hadn't questioned me on that fact, because the mere thought of living with my best friend is preposterous. She lives with her family still, her parents, her twin tween brothers, and her three-year-old baby sister. Their house is like an episode of 'Full House' and Nellie constantly complains, wanting to move out, but she doesn't have the money to.

"Rox, you need to get it over with," Chad tells me, sitting down next to me.

"I know, but I'm scared he's going to crack it."

"We'll cross that bridge when we come to it. Just call him and arrange the date as we talked about."

Still my Girl

"Ok," I reply, standing up, turning my back to Chad so I
don't laugh. Pacing my room I dial my brother's number
and he answers straight away.

"Hey, little sis. What's up?"

"Hi, Jessie. I um...wanted to ask you something."

"What? Do you need money? Are you ok?"

"I'm fine. Great actually, and no I don't need money."

"Then what Roxanne?"

"I was wondering if you and Teagan would like to go on a
double date with me and my new boyfriend."

He acts all protective, blurting out, "Since when do you
have a boyfriend?"

"Um, it's new. And I'm nervous about going on a date with
him," I tell my brother, stupidly turning around to look at
Chad who's trying to stifle his laughter.

I wave at him to stop, trying not to laugh myself.

"Ok, so what were you thinking?"

Chad mouths, 'Pizza at Barney's' to me. I give him a
thumbs up. "Um, maybe pizza's at Barney's?"

"Right. So when?"

"Saturday at seven pm?"

"Should be sweet. I'll text you if it's not ok with Teags."

"Ok, see you then big brother."

"Bye Rox. Be careful." He hangs up, and I gulp from the
warning in his tone.

Chad has burst into laughter and throwing my phone on
the bed, I run to him and push him down on the bed.

"Hey girlfriend," he says with a smirk. His sexy smirk that shows his double dimple. I laugh, and kiss the dimple, and he lets out a hot whimper that makes my core throb.

"So, my sexy girlfriend, will I be able to kiss you on this date?"

"Um, no, hot boyfriend, you won't, but you can kiss me now."

"Oh, and what else can I do?" he asks, licking his lips. He doesn't give me a moment to answer his question before he's kissing me, licking my lips to deepen the kiss that already has my body craving his touch. Pulling back, I lick his lips and whisper against them, "You. can. Lick. my. Pussy."

He moans, deep, his chest vibrating against mine, and the contact makes my nipples rise to attention. He slides a hand down between our bodies, straight into my shorts and knickers.

"Mmm, sexy girlfriend, you're so wet," he taunts, rubbing his finger over my clit. "You want an Aussie kiss?"

I nod, giving him a cheeky smile.

"Then take off those skimpy little shorts, and get up here to ride my face, baby."

His words make my core throb, and sitting up I pull my shorts down, wiggling out of them and kicking them off my at my feet. Chad licks his lips, taking in my lacy knickers.

"Get up here, baby," Chad teases.

Still my Girl

Scooting up his abs I sit over his chin, my clit right at his lips. He darts his tongue out to lick my bud through the lace, and it sends a delightful shiver through me.

"Touch yourself, baby. Pull those knickers aside for me."

I obey his request, feeling hella turned on. His tongue is inside me, licking my pussy like he can't get enough. He's murmuring and moaning and it's turning me on so much. His lips press kisses to my body, sucking on my sensitive bud. He stops for a moment, and I move back a little.

"Ride my face, Rox. Rub your pretty pussy all over my face."

I feel my core clench with his words. And again move up, rubbing up and down over his chin and lips, whilst he licks and kisses me. It feels fucking incredible.

Behind me I can feel his hand stroking his dick, matching the stroke of his hand with the stroke of his tongue licking me.

The pleasure is so intense, I feel my whole body starting to tremble, and I bare down on Chad's lips, screaming out, "Oh fuck! I'm coming!"

My orgasm is shattering, an intense wave and Chad laps it up before I scoot back down so my crotch is in line with his dick. He moves his hand away and I rock over his length, making him come hard with a bellowing, "Fuck! Rox!"

I lean down, kissing him, tasting myself on his plump lips.

"Another first," I murmur against his lips.

"Damn Rox. I love giving you all your firsts."

"Yeah, well I love you."

"Back at you gorgeous. I love you so much Rox. But now I think we need some food."

"Yeah, like what?"

"Chinese takeaway."

"Sounds perfect. I'm going to go have a shower," I tell him, getting up from the bed.

"Ooo, can I join you?" Chad asks, standing up and grabbing me around the waist.

"No," I protest, wiggling out of his arms. "We'll never eat if you do."

"Fair point. Go shower, baby. I'll order the food."

He slaps me playfully on the butt as I walk out to the bathroom.

I'm worried that Jessie is going to warn me away from Chad, or worse. And I can't stand thinking about that. Being with Chad, being his girl is better than I ever imagined and I'm worried it's going to be all over when we're just beginning.

24. Chad

Parking my fiesta next to Rox's jeep I take a deep breath in to quell the anxiousness I'm feeling. I'm so in love with Roxanne, but I don't Jessie is going to like us being together, especially the fact that I took her innocence away.

Rox had already gone in to meet her brother, claiming that her date—her new boyfriend—had stood her up and my plan was to saunter in, act all nonchalant and feel the vibe out to see if telling Jessie is the right thing. He needs to know. Rox is his little sister, and he's always been over the top protective of her. The fact he'd kicked her out and has barely spoken to these past couple of months surprises me.

Getting out of the car, I lock it and walk into the Barney's. It's packed with people and when I'm asked if I need a table I spot Rox sitting across from Jessie and Teagan in a booth at the back. I nod to the waitress and point to them. She lets me go through and sauntering up to the table I stop, grinning and pressing my hands against the tabletop.

111

"Well, well, fancy running into the Donaghey's here."

Jessie scoffs at me, his eyes darting to Rox who's trying not to grin.

"Not even going to say hello Jessman, or offer me a seat to join you."

Again he scoffs, looking at Rox protectively.

I smile at her. "Scoot over Rox."

She scoots over in the booth, and sneakily runs her hand up my thigh, towards my dick. I gasp, folding my hands in front of me, resting them on the table.

"So, Jessman, Teags, how are things? You know after you kicked me to the curb like a stray dog?"

Teagan smiles at me, her stupid sickly sweet, butter doesn't melt in my damn mouth smile. I honestly don't know why I was ever attracted to her.

"Things are good, Chad. We're getting married in a couple months," Teagan coos at me.

"That's ripper. Congrats," I tell her, looking at Jessie for some kind of reaction. He looks like someone has put a firecracker up his arse. His face is flushed red hot and he's balling his fists.

I look at Rox, who looks like she's on the verge of tears. I lean in closer to her, brushing my lips against her ear and whispering, "I think I should go, baby. We'll tell him later." She grabs my hand, squeezing it before I get up. I want to kiss her goodbye, but that would likely give me a punch to the face so instead, I turn to walk out.

Still my Girl

I barely make it a metre before Jessie has stood up, and he shoves me in the back. I turn back to look at him, and he's seething.

"You got a problem, Jessie?" I ask, taunting him, about to raise my fists at him.

"Yeah I've got a problem, Chad," he drawls angrily.

"And that is? I was just leaving."

"No, you aren't mate. You're going to tell me what's really going on here."

"Nothing, Jessie. You're just being a right wanker and making a damn scene."

"Right, a scene. So you're telling me nothing, absolutely fucking nothing is going on with you and my sister?"

I feel the knot in my stomach intensify, twisting up when I gulp and reply, "No, there is nothing going on with me and Rox."

"Do you think I'm fucking blind and stupid?"

"No, I said nothing of the sort."

"Of course you've got nothing to say. You're hiding something."

I gulp again, feeling completely and utterly tongue-tied and stupefied. I want to blurt out insulting words.

"So what if I am Jessie? I'm not the dickwad who takes his girl back after she cheats on him."

He raises his fist, about to lay into me, when Rox stands up and steps in front of me.

"Get out of the way Roxanne!" Jessie seethes at his sister.

"No! Not until you step down from laying into my boyfriend."

Jessie's mouth falls open, as does mine.

"What the fuck Roxanne? What did you just fucking say?"

"You heard me, Jessie. Chad is my boyfriend. And I've been living with him, not Nellie."

He pushes her aside—turning to me again—anger flaring in his eyes and nostrils. He's possessed like a bull about to charge.

"You arsehole! What don't you get about staying away from my sister?"

"I...I...never hurt her. I fucking love her, Jessman."

"Pfft, don't give me that shit, Chad."

Rox tries to say something next to me, but he gestures for her to zip it. I try to pull her against my side, but Jessie is coming at me, his hands pushing into my chest.

"I'm not shitting you, Jessie."

"Whatever, I don't believe you, seriously."

"Fine, man, suit yourself. You clearly don't know what love is being with a cheating skank."

He's still seething, not replying but suddenly punching me right in the cheek. He shoves his hands into my chest, making me stumble backwards.

I raise my fists up to fight back but stop myself. I need to fight for Rox, but again this isn't the place for that.

Before Jessie can hit me again, I turn to walk away.

Still my Girl

Rox follows me, about to grab my hand when he pulls her back.

"Don't even think about going with him Roxanne. You're coming home with me."

She screams out, "No! I want to go with Chad. I love him."

"Roxanne, I will not tell you twice. Let him go."

Rox looks at me, standing at the door. I can see her heart is breaking when she mouths, *'I'm sorry Chad. I love you'* to me.

I blow her a kiss, walking out the door to my car.

And getting in to drive home—without Rox—tears fall down my cheeks. I'm fucking crying because I've lost my girl when things were only just beginning.

25. Roxanne

My heart shatters, watching Chad walk out the door of Barney's. Jessie tries to comfort me—to pull me into a hug —but I brush him off. He's the reason tears are streaming down my cheeks and my heart is walking out the door with the only guy I've ever loved.

It was always Chad, and it will always be Chad.

I want to run after him, but my feet are glued to the floor. I'm literally stuck in place and falling apart.

Teagan stands up, and steps in front of me. "Are you ok, Roxy?" she asks me, sweetly.

I gulp, my mouth dry and no words come out, just wretched sobs. She comfortingly wraps her arms around me, and even though it feels kinda odd I cry into her shoulder. I feel her look up at Jessie, and she whispers words to him, "I can't believe you, Jessie."

"What Teags? He's clearly playing my sister."

"You don't know that." She takes a step back from him then, and I force myself to move and grab my bag.

Still my Girl

Jessie gives me dagger eyes. "Where do you think you're going, Roxanne?"

"To my car, and home."

"No, Teagan will go with you. You're coming back to ours."

"Fine," I huff, brushing past them both, and rushing out to my jeep. Part of me is hoping Chad is still here, and I can hitch back with him, screw my brother and my car.

But Chad's fiesta is nowhere in sight.

I quickly jump into the jeep and turn the engine over. I'm about to speed off, straight back to Chad's when the passenger door is yanked open and Teagan climbs in, latching her seatbelt and smiling at me.

It makes my stomach lurch. I have no choice but to go to theirs and I nearly jump out of my seat when my brother is driving up my arse, honking his horn at me. I pull out of the carpark into traffic, focusing on the drive back to my brothers' and not the hella awkward silence in the car.

"I'm sorry Roxy."

I feel like a bitch with my reply, "Whatever, Teagan. Please don't pretend you care right now."

She gulps loudly, muttering something I can't understand.

Arriving back at Jessie's fifteen minutes later, Teagan doesn't get out of the car until Jessie is at my door.

He yanks it open, turns the ignition off and pockets my keys.

"You're staying here tonight, Roxanne."

"Fine," I huff again, getting out of the jeep and following them both inside. My blood is absolutely boiling over with anger.

My brother is being a complete arsehole.

"So, are you going to tell me the truth?" Jessie asks, standing in the doorway of my old room.

"Why? What does it matter? It's not like you care."

"I do care, Roxanne. Because I care, I want the truth."

"Fine, the truth is I found a roommate ad, and I didn't know it was Chad until the day I moved in. And we've been together pretty much ever since."

"And by together you mean what exactly?"

"I mean together, Jessie. Everything. The whole shebang."

"So you slept with him?"

"Yes," I reply turning to walk towards the bed.

Jessie follows me.

"You can't be serious, Roxanne. How could you be so stupid?"

"Sleeping with Chad wasn't a stupid mistake like you seem to think it is Jessie," I chastise my brother, crossing my arms over my chest to not lash out at him.

"I'm in love with him. And that's what you do when you love someone. You give them everything."

"Well, regardless. You're not to see him again. He might have been my best mate, but he's not the guy for you."

Still my Girl

"Whatever, Jessie," I snap, turning my back to him and pulling back the covers of the bed. "Leave me alone, please."

He walks out without another word, and I yank off my leggings, and skater dress, climbing into the cold bed in my underwear.

I miss Chad, miss feeling his arms wrapped around me. No place has ever felt more like home, and I'm empty without him.

Drifting to sleep, tears cascading down my cheeks I think about a way to see him, if only for a minute.

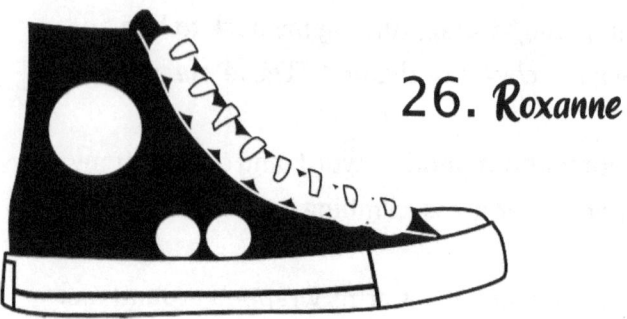

26. Roxanne

Feeling like I'm under house arrest, I stumble into the kitchen, bleary-eyed because I barely slept. Jessie is in the kitchen, making french toast and coffee.

"Morning Roxanne," he greets me with a to chipper tone for so early in the morning.

"Morning," I groan, yawning loudly and stretching.

"So I spoke to Teags last night, and she asked about your clothes and stuff."

"Yeah, what about them?"

"Well, you don't really have any left here."

"What are you saying?"

"I was thinking we could drive over together, and get them."

My eyes boggle at his suggestion, but I'm a touch confused.

"So you're going to take me to Chad's to get my stuff?"

"Yeah," he replies, handing me a plate of french toast.

"And what's the catch?"

"No catch, per se, but we'll go in with you if that's what you're asking."

Still my Girl

Of course, I can't be trusted.

"Ok, I guess. I'll need to text Chad to let him know. Or you'll have to give me my keys back."

"I'm not stupid, Roxanne. I already text him. And you're not getting your keys back."

"Seriously, Jessie. Why are you being like this? I honestly don't understand what you have against Chad."

He gets suddenly defensive, balling his fists angrily.

"He's not the guy for you Roxy. He's always taken advantage of you, and put you in situations you shouldn't have been in. And I don't trust him to not hurt you."

"What are you talking about?"

"Has he told you anything about why he barely spoke to either of us after he left?"

"No, but what does it matter now?"

"Because he's a player, Roxanne. He'll hurt you. And I'm not going to let that happen."

"Maybe he's changed."

"People don't change, Roxanne," he tells me, swallowing hard.

He needs to heed his own advice. But I don't tell him that, instead I take a bite of my french toast, carrying the plate to the bedroom to get dressed.

An hour later, we're in Jessie's car, heading over to—Chad's —my house. I'm hoping for a minute to myself and hoping like hell that Chad is home. It's not even been twenty-four hours, but I miss him so much it hurts.

As we pull up outside, my heart is hammering in my chest, and I bound out of the car, straight to the front door. Jessie and Teagan follow me in and stand in the lounge room completely dumbfounded. I honestly don't know why they're acting so weird. Jessie is about to follow me down the hallway, but I stop him with a hand against his chest.

"Please, Jessie. Let me have a minute. I need some space for a minute."

My brother sighs, worriedly.

"Fine, be as quick as you can."

I head to my room, noticing Chad's door is ajar and soft music wafts from his room.

From my wardrobe, I start packing my clothes back into my suitcase and almost jump out of my skin when I turn to find Chad standing next to me.

"Hey Rox. I missed you baby."

"I missed you too, but I have to be quick. Jessie and Teagan are waiting for me."

"Yeah, I know. But I just had to see you," he says with a smirk. "You're still my girl, Rox. I love you."

"I love you too, Chad. But we can't be together."

He doesn't reply, instead pulls me into a hug, squeezing me tightly for a moment before pulling back and kissing me hard. My heart is pounding in my chest, my whole body humming with desire for Chad when he pushes me against the wall at the back of my walk-in wardrobe.

His kiss is frantic, our tongues dancing together. His hand reaches under my skater dress, straight into my knickers, and finding that I'm soaked he groans against my lips breaking the kiss.

"Fuck, Rox. I want you so bad."

"Quickie goodbye fuck?" I ask, smirking at him.

"Oh yeah, baby. But not goodbye," he taunts, yanking his grey trackies down. His dick is already rock hard, and he's commando and ready to slam into me.

Smiling at him I slip my knickers down to my knees, and grabbing me around the waist he spears into me. Kissing me zealously he licks my lips, his tongue dancing with mine, the pace matching his hard thrusts inside my pussy. And god does it feel good, so dirty, naughty and arousing.

I tear my mouth from his with a moan. He claps his hand over my mouth, thrusting harder into my pussy.

I lick his palm, and he groans, biting down on his lip to suppress his moans when we crash over the edge together.

"Fuck Rox, that was hot. I love you, so fucking much, baby," he whispers, his eyes locked on mine.

"I love you too, Chad," I reply, kissing him again before we pull up our daks.

"Want some help to pack your stuff?" he asks softly.

"I'm just packing basics. I'm coming back, I promise."

"Ok, baby," he replies, winking and helping me shove some of my clothes into the suitcase.

Once it's full I wheel it out behind me, stopping a moment at the door to give Chad one last kiss—one last hug—that I don't want to break.

Walking out into the lounge room, Jessie gives me dagger eyes glaring at me like I've got my head screwed on backwards. I follow him out, hanging back a little bit with Teagan. She elbows me in the side.

"Did you fuck him?" she whispers in my ear before we get in the car.

I find myself nodding, and cursing myself because I hope she doesn't snitch to my brother. But her smile tells me my secret is safe and she laughs pretending to zip her lips as we slide into the car.

I turn my gaze to look out the window, so Jessie won't see the tears stinging my eyes. I told Chad I'd be back, and I'm hoping I can keep that promise.

27. Roxanne

In the few weeks since Jessie forced me to leave Chad's I've been down in the dumps, and not even being able to text Chad because Jessie decided I couldn't be trusted with my phone, has only made matters worse.

Teagan has been acting mega weird, trying to be my best friend when I really don't know whether to trust her.

Having to help her with wedding planning is further cementing my horrid mood, but I'm doing it to help take my mind off things.

Pulling up in front of the bridal boutique I cut the engine of the jeep, and we climb out together.

Teagan smiles at me, as I follow her inside.

"I'm so excited for you to see the bridesmaid dress. It's going to look so great on you."

"If you think so," I reply when she goes up to the counter.

I take a moment to glance around the room. It's filled to the brim with all sorts of wedding gowns, and it makes me a little teary.

A moment later Teagan comes back over to me, and I follow her into the fitting rooms at the back of the boutique.

We sit on the couch in the middle of the room, and I sniff back sobs. I don't know what is getting to me so much about being here.

"Are you ok?" Teagan asks me, lightly touching my arm. "We can come back if you're sick or something."

"No, I'm fine. I um...it's nothing. It's just silly thoughts."

"Tell me, please Roxanne. I'm here if you need to talk."

"I miss Chad," I declare, feeling the hot tears break through.

"He means a lot to you huh?" Teagan asks me again with a sweet smile.

"Yeah, I love him. I always have, but Jessie can't see past the Chad he knows," I tell her, wiping my sleeve across my cheeks.

"I get that. What happened between us was a big mistake, and I'm so glad Jessie forgave me and proposed."

"Yeah, me too. I'm glad you guys are happy."

Again she smiles sweetly at me. I'm still feeling wary of her, knowing that she kissed Chad. But I don't get to question her or say anything more, as the assistant comes out with a flowing dusty pink chiffon gown.

Teagan squeals in delight, jumping up from the couch to run over to the assistant and grab it from her. She holds it up to me.

Still my Girl

"So do you like it?"

"It's lovely," I reply, reaching out to touch the fabric.

"Yay!" Teagan squeals excitedly, handing it to me. "Go try it on."

I slip behind the curtain, and strip out of my leggings—and Chad's hoodie—which I secretly took from the place I'd hidden it in my wardrobe after we slept together.

I'd only worn it around home until today, and it still smelt like Chad—earthy, manly and sexy—and it was both comforting and upsetting.

Carefully I unzip the invisible zip at the side of the dress and step into it, slipping the thick straps over my shoulders before I do it up. It does look stunning. I've never worn a dress like this before, and it makes me feel like a princess. The straps are wide and it dips at the front into a sweetheart neckline where it gathers around the bust, before falling into a wave of flowing fabric.

Opening the curtain I step out to Teagan and the sales assistant and they both smile.

"Oh, Roxanne. It looks perfect."

"Really?"

"Yes, and with the right heels it's the perfect length."

She jumps at me, hugging me awkwardly.

"Go get changed again, so I can pay for it. I have an idea about your man."

I quickly get changed again, and after paying for the dress we leave, heading to a coffee shop a few doors down.

Sitting down ten minutes later with coffee's in hand, Teagan suddenly says, "So I was thinking I'll sneak a lookie at Jessie's phone and get Chad's number."

"Um, ok, but how is that going to help?" I ask, worriedly. I don't know if Teagan having Chad's number is a good idea.

"I'll text him, and tell him where to meet you at uni after class."

"Um, ok, I guess."

"I promise I won't do anything with his number. Seems pretty clear to me that he loves you, Roxanne. And I love Jessie. Just let me help you. It's the least I can do."

"Ok, sounds like a plan," I reply with a laugh, before sipping my coffee. A plan that I honestly don't know will even work. If I had my way I'd just go to Chad's house—my house—and barge in to kiss him and have my way with him, but I don't trust Teagan to not blab to Jessie.

Even with her offer, I still feel like she has a hidden agenda.

We both quickly finish our drinks and head back to their house.

I'm feeling giddy at the prospect of seeing Chad again. I only wish it could be somewhere more private, but hopefully, that might happen soon. Right now even just being at the same place at the same time would be better than anything. I'm still thinking about our secret wardrobe fuck—the day I had to leave—but even though the

Still my Girl

memory is still clear in my mind, the feeling of his kiss on my lips is fading. And I want that feeling back.

28. Chad

Getting a text message from Teagan about meeting Rox at Uni definitely had me wary. I'd tried messaging Rox but got no reply. And Teagan was a vindictive bitch, so walking towards the place I'm supposed to meet Rox I'm fully expecting to see Teagan instead.

But turning the corner towards the side of the main building I find Rox leaning against the wall. She looks stunning—her long brown hair down around her shoulders—wearing black leggings and my missing hoodie.

Spotting me walking up to her she smiles, and it makes my heart pound in my chest.

She runs to me, wrapping her arms around my body in a hug. I wrap my arms around her tightly, squeezing her and lifting her feet off the ground.

"I've missed you, Rox," I tell her, putting her feet back down. I kiss her forehead and grab her hand to drag her around the corner, away from prying eyes.

Standing against the wall, I pull her against my body.

Still my Girl

I'm aching for her. And smile when she says, "I've missed you too, but we can't...Jessie is hovering."

"I know Rox, but not seeing you is torture. My dick needs you."

"Haha, Chad. I love you, but I have to go."

Again I hug her, slipping my hand under the hoodie and up her torso. Reaching her tits, I find she's braless. And it makes my dick stir again.

"Damn, Rox, baby," I groan, brushing my thumbs over her nipples. She squirms and murmurs, before closing the distance between us and kissing me. The kiss is frantic and hot, with Rox grinding against my straining dick, fucking me with clothes on. She's moaning against my lips and breaks the kiss breathless.

"I love you to Roxanne," I tell her softly, kissing her again, hard. She licks my lips to deepen the kiss, and it makes my dick throb, even more so when she bites my lips, taking charge of the kiss.

I so wish we weren't out in a public place—in the middle of the day—because I want to fuck her hard right now. Moaning I tear my mouth from hers.

"Fuck, Rox, I want to fuck you so bad right now."

She giggles. "I know. But I have to go."

"I know, Rox," I reply when she stretches up to kiss my cheek.

"I love you, Chad, and I'm keeping my promise to you."

"I know," I reply as she walks away—taking my heart with her—leaving me feeling overwhelmed and thinking of ways to be with her again.

I should have asked if she had a phone or something because getting to kiss her again has made my whole body ache. I have no idea what to do because life without Roxanne is no life at all.

She's my girl.

And I need to think of some way to show her and her idiot brother—my ex-best friend—that she will always be my girl.

29. Roxanne

Walking away from Chad, my whole body is aching to run straight back into his arms. I miss him so much, it hurts.

I feel silly for doing what my brother says, but I don't want to disappoint him, nor lose my brother because he's always been there for me.

Chad had as well until he moved away, and what my brother keeps telling me about Chad's past does bother me a little. I make a mental note to probe Jessie about it more, walking away from Chad, watching him step away from the corner to look at me again.

I'm about to turn around to run back into Chad's arms, but I bump straight into my brother. He scowls at me, steadying me and stopping me from moving with his hands on my shoulders.

"Hey, Roxanne," he says harshly. I hate when he uses my full name, lacing his voice with parental concern. I don't even know what my parents would think about Chad and I. They'd always loved him when we were kids, and very nearly adopted him and his little sister, but his foster parents got the approval instead. I shake the thoughts of the past away, not wanting to think about what could have been.

"Was that Chad I just saw you with?" Jessie asks, still holding my shoulders square. I pull away from his grip on me.

"No, you're dreaming Jessie," I snap, turning away from my brother's intense stare.

"I told you to stay away from him Roxanne," he seethes at me, anger flaring in his eyes because it's clear I'm lying to him. Jessie has a built-in lie detector, he can always see straight through any bullshit I try to spin.

"Why Jessie? Why is Chad not good enough for me?" I question him, my hands on my hips to try and show some defiance.

"Because he'll hurt you, Roxanne. He's never been with one girl long enough to develop any feelings and you're my little sister," Jessie explains.

"Yeah, well, things are different with me. He loves me." Jessie scoffs. "And you actually believe him?"

"Yes. I love him too," I tell my brother, again with defiance in my tone.

"Seriously Roxanne," my brother snaps, sighing. "Let him go."

I stomp my foot, anger flaring inside me.

"You can't stop me from seeing him!"

"I'm going to try," Jessie muses, about to walk away. "Did you drive today?" he asks.

"Nah, got the tram."

"Great. I'll meet you back here to take you home after my class," he tells me.

"Ok, whatever," I reply heading towards the coffee shop after Jessie leaves.

On the walk there I'm thinking about ways to see Chad. I should get a new phone, but I don't really miss having one. Life seems so much simpler without being on social media every minute. It just makes it hard to keep in touch with my friends and my parents.

Walking into the coffee shop, I spot Nellie sitting with our other friend Maria. She waves at me, and waving back I quickly order my coffee before going to sit with her and Maria.

"Hey, Roxy. How're things?" Maria asks, smiling at me.

"Could be better."

"Yeah, why's that?"

"I can't be with my boyfriend."

"Oh yeah, Nel was just telling me you hooked up with Chad."

"Yeah, but we can't be together, because my brother is an arsehole."

"Why don't you just go back to Chad's house?" Nellie asks when my coffee is bought over to the table. I take a sip of the latte before I reply, "Because Jessie will come over—

again—to drag me back home. He thinks Chad isn't good enough for me, but honestly won't tell me why."

"Well, Jessie is being a prick, Roxy. Chad loves you, and he treats you like a princess," Nellie says sweetly.

"I know, but there's no changing Jessie's mind. No matter what I say about how Chad feels or how he treats me, Jessie won't listen."

"Sucks, Roxy. I hope your brother comes around," Maria interjects.

"Thanks, Maria. I do too. I hate having to sneak around to see Chad, and I miss being with him so much."

"Yeah, that's understandable," Nellie says, giggling. "You never did tell me about losing your v-card to him."

I feel myself blush, and quickly sip the rest of my coffee.

"It was amazing, Nel. And so has every time since then been. He makes my whole body feel warm, alive. I love him so much."

"You guys are meant to be. You've always been Chad's girl."

"Yeah, I think I've always loved him," I tell my best friend with a smile. "Anyway, I have to go to meet Jessie. I'll see you tomorrow."

Nellie stands up at the same time as I do, giving me a hug before I leave. I'm so glad to have such amazing friends, who can see how perfect Chad and I are together. I just hope that my brother comes around soon too because life without Chad is just monotonous and my heart aches.

30. *Chad*

A month or so later

In the last couple of months, I've barely spoken to Rox and only seen her a handful of times. I can't fucking stand it anymore. I need to see her, need to get her back no matter the consequences.

She'd thankfully gotten her phone back, so I send her a text telling her I'm coming over. She doesn't reply—but I don't care—I'm going over to see her regardless.

Getting to the Donaghey's front door again—and knocking—a rush of deja vu hits me, making me laugh and think back to when I crashed back into their lives. When I came face to face with Rox again and fell for her, hook, line and sinker to the bottom of the ocean this time.

I'm hoping Rox opens the door, but I wouldn't be so lucky. With a huff, Jessie opens the door, staring at me like I'm the devil standing on his doorstep and have come to take his soul.

"Hey, Jessie," I greet him with a smile, hoping he won't bite my head off.

"What the fuck are you doing here, Chad?" he bellows at me, not even saying hello.

I gulp. "Coming to see Rox," I tell him.

"Yeah, she's not here. And she doesn't want to see you."

"Bullshit, Jessie. More like you don't want her to see me." I push my hands into his chest, crossing the threshold of his front doorstep. "But I don't care what you want anymore. I'm in love with Rox, and I'm going to be with her whether you approve of us being together or not."

He doesn't reply, just stares daggers at me when I push past him, straight to Rox's room.

She's sitting on her bed reading, and I just watch her a moment. My heart is hammering in my chest. She looks so beautiful and I'm caught between watching her and wanting to rush over and wrap my arms around her before kissing her.

I'm about to do that when Jessie steps up behind me, tapping my back.

"You telling me the truth? You're not going to break my baby sisters heart?"

"I'm telling you the truth, Jessman. I honestly love her, so hard."

He ponders my words a moment, scratching his head and running a hand through his dark hair.

Still my Girl

"Fine, I can see you love her. You wouldn't be here if you didn't." He smirks at me then, lacing his tone with a threat, "But if you ever hurt her you'll be six feet under in ten seconds."

"Noted. And I'll never hurt her. She's my girl Jessman. Always has been, always will be my girl."

Roxy looks up from her book then, smiling wide when she sees me talking to her brother. Jumping off the bed, she meets me halfway across the room. Our arms wrap around each other in a tight hug, her feet lifting off the floor. She kisses me softly and Jessie laughs from the doorway of her bedroom.

"How about no full PDA in front of me, yeah?" he says with a smirk.

Breaking the kiss with Rox, I apologise jovially, "Sorry, brother in law."

Again Jessie laughs, his tone jovial when he replies, "Yeah, wait a bit for that Chad. I'm only just getting used to my baby sister having a boyfriend, and being with my best mate at that."

With an arm around Rox, we head back to the doorway of her bedroom.

"Sorry man. Are we good?" I ask Jessie, hoping things can go back to normal between us because I miss my best mate a helluva lot.

"Yeah. Never better, best man," he jeers.

"Sweet, man. So you're really getting married, huh?"

"Yeah, and having you as my best man is all I want."
I look to Rox—smiling—next to me. "And you're the maid of honour, baby?"
"Yep, that I am," she coos, smiling.
"Sounds ripper. But right now, if your brother doesn't mind we have some catching up to do."
Jessie laughs. "I don't need to know. Maybe head back to yours. We'll catch up later in the week."
"No worries," I reply, taking Rox's hand and walking out of the house.
She can't stop smiling when she gets into the fiesta and all the way back to our house.

Back at our house, twenty minutes later I drag Rox inside, kissing her the moment we step inside the front door.
She climbs into my arms wanting to get as close as possible. It's clear she's missed me as much as I've missed her. Her breath fans against my ear when she breaks the kiss, and she whispers in my ear, "Fuck me, please Chad."
I groan, her words making my dick throb.
I contemplate taking her to the bedroom—but it seems so far away—and the couch is right next to us.
"Chad, please, now," Rox begs huskily.
I throw her down on the couch—and with her eyes locked on mine—she starts to strip off her clothes.

Still my Girl

Her t-shirt first, then her bra. I yank off my t-shirt and grey trackies, and I'm naked in front of her.

She murmurs, biting her lip and grabs my waist, pulling me down on top of her.

Kissing her I murmur against her lips, "You've still got clothes on baby."

She bucks her hips against me, and hooking my fingers in the side of her leggings I yank them down to find she's wearing a g-string underneath.

"Damn, Rox. A g under leggings is so damn sexy."

She giggles, grabbing my cheeks to pull my lips back to hers for a hungry kiss. I've missed being skin to skin, lips locked. Being so close to Rox sets my whole body alight. Breaking the kiss, I start trailing kisses over her body, as usual tracing her scar with my tongue.

Stopping before I reach her pussy I look up at her smiling. She gives me a questioning look.

"What's wrong?"

"Just thinking about how much I love you. And how long I've loved you."

"What do you mean?" she asks, wide-eyed, a little breathless.

Touching her scar again, rubbing my finger over it softly she murmurs.

"I think I've loved you since the day you got this scar. I wanted to help you and take care of you so much that day. And when Jessie pushed me away it really hurt."

"Oh Chad," she murmurs, sitting up and kissing me sweetly. "I've loved you since before I knew what love was."

"Aww, Roxanne. I love you so much, baby," I tell her stretching over her body and kissing her, plunging my rock hard dick inside her.

She whimpers against my lips, her hips rising up to meet my thrusts.

Breaking the kiss when I slow my thrusts, Rox whispers huskily, "I love you Chad. I want to ride your dick."

I don't say anything, except pull her up into my arms as I sit back on the couch. My dick is still inside her pussy, and she straddles me, lifting her pussy off my dick for a moment before impaling herself down on me hard and deep.

"Oh, god, Chad," she cries out. "So good, fuck, so good."

She bounces up and down on my dick, stretching her body back, and fisting her hair. Her body is on display for me, and she looks fucking beautiful, so sexy. Reaching up I palm her tits in my hands, and she moans loudly, bouncing up and down harder and faster on my dick.

"Chad, fuck, fuck! I'm gonna come."

"Oh yeah baby, come on my dick," I roar, my hands sliding down her body to grip her hips as she loses herself in the pleasure.

My dick is throbbing inside her—her pussy clenching around me—with her impending release. She starts to

Still my Girl

tremble—baring down on my hips—her breath coming out in pants when she explodes over me in an intense rush.
I pull her down over my chest for a kiss.
"Baby, that was so hot. Can I take you from behind now?"
She sits up, brushing her hair back, and nods, biting down on her lip. Her nervousness makes me chuckle.
"Another first, baby."
When she gets up off my lap, I take her against my chest, kissing her zealously. I love giving her all her first experiences when it comes to sex. It turns me on so much. Breaking the kiss, she whispers against my lips, "All my firsts for you, Chad."
"Oh baby, you have no idea how much that turns me on."
She reaches down and grabs my dick in her fists.
"I'm not sure about that, baby. Your dick is hard as for me."
"Oh, Rox, did you just call me baby?"
She blushes, biting her lip before she moans, "Baby, take me."
I groan, feeling like I'm gonna come just from her sexy innuendo.
"Bend over the couch, baby," I request, my eyes locked on hers. She follows the direction, putting her hands down on the couch and her arse in the air, towards me.
Lifting her head and looking back at me, she teases, "Fuck me, baby. Take me, Chad."
Groaning, I grip her hips and shove inside her pussy.

Caz May

She meets my thrusts, rocking her arse back against me. It feels incredible and Rox's moans are driving me wild.

I grab a fist of her hair, yanking it back when I pound into her harder, faster and deeper. "Fuck, Chad, fuck me!" she calls out—stretching up—her back meeting my chest.

Her lips crash against mine in a fierce kiss, and I wrap my arms around her, reaching down to tease her clit with my thumb.

She moans against my mouth, taking my tongue with hers, whilst I rock my pelvis against her arse. I can feel my release building from my balls, and can feel Rox starting to tremble with her release building as well.

Breaking the kiss, I whisper against her lips, "Come for me, Rox, baby."

She lets out a lascivious moan, her whole body shaking with my final thrust into her pussy. I feel my release shoot inside her, filling her as she clenches around me taking every last drop.

Pulling out, I turn her body around to face me.

"That was incredible Rox. I love you so fucking much, baby."

"Another first," she murmurs, kissing me softly, but passionately. And against my lips she whispers, "I love you Chad. I'm your girl."

I murmur, breaking the kiss and staring at her, straight into her sweet brown eyes.

Still my Girl

"Oh yeah, Rox. You were my girl when we were kids, and you're still my girl."

She smiles kissing me quickly, before she steps out of my arms to head to the kitchen.

I watch her walking away—naked—and chuckle when she bends down to get the milk out of the fridge.

"Mmm, damn," I curse, heading to the kitchen.

"What, baby?"

"Nothing. Just enjoying watching you walk around our house naked."

"Oh," she mutters with a laugh.

"It's sexy. Maybe we should make a rule that clothes are not required when at home."

"Oh really?" She taunts me, stepping into my personal space to kiss me again. "And why would I agree to that?"

"Because you want me. And if I'm naked you can have me whenever you want, baby."

She laughs, and it's so damn sexy my dick stirs again.

I'll never get enough of Roxanne Donaghey.

"Likewise, Chad. But right now I need food, and then maybe we can have dessert in bed."

I chuckle at her dirty innuendo.

"When did you get so dirty, Rox?"

"When you kissed me the first time, baby."

"Oh, so when you were thirteen?"

"Yeah, when you left I looked up all sorts of dirty things, because I'd never felt the way you made me feel."

"Aww, Roxanne. That's so cute, baby. Come here and show me how that kiss made you feel."

Before I can think, she's pressing her body against mine and taking my mouth in a desperate kiss full of longing. There's no way I'm ever letting her go again.

31. *Chad*

Rox comes crashing into the house—after uni—with a look on her face like she's had the day from hell. She stops in the kitchen, sighing when she sits down on the breakfast bar stool.

"Hey, baby," I greet her with a smile, holding out a cup of coffee to her. "Bad day?"

"The worst. I swear Professor Flip the Pony has it in for me."

I snort, spitting out my mouthful of coffee. "Professor what?"

"Flip the Pony. Well, Fliliponi. But he's a dick, so we gave him that nickname."

"Oh right. So what did Professor Flip the Pony do?" I ask her, taking another sip of coffee and trying not to laugh.

"He calls on me for every damn question, and then when I'm wrong he chastises me and corrects me. And everyone stares and sniggers."

"Oh, baby. I'm sorry, that's mega shit. Can you transfer out of his class?"

"No," she replies with a long sigh, downing the rest of her coffee before she jumps off the stool.

"Oh, double shit. Guess you'll just have to stick it out then."

"Yeah," she grumbles, looking so sad I want to kick Professor Flip the Pony in the fucking nuts.

"I'm gonna go have a shower," she mumbles, heading down the hallway.

I follow her, stopping her outside the bathroom.

"Chad, please. I just want to forget about today."

"I know baby, which is exactly why I'm taking you out for the night."

Her eyes light up, and she stretches up to kiss me softly. "Ooo, where to?"

"It's a surprise but you should wear something sexy."

She giggles, sauntering into the bathroom, and lifting her t-shirt over her head.

"So my birthday suit, then?"

I'm watching her, watching her taking off every piece of clothing. And chuckle when she's standing naked in front me, taunting me with a hand on her hip. "You naked is damn sexy, Rox. But you will need clothes for this occasion."

"If you insist, baby," she taunts, stepping into the shower and starting the water. Again I watch her, as she starts to lather her body with soap. Watching her is so fucking arousing, my dick is screaming in my trackies.

148

Still my Girl

"Fuck it," I mumble, shoving my trackies and jocks to the floor. Yanking my t-shirt off, I slide the shower screen across and step in, wrapping Rox in my arms.

Kissing the water droplets from her neck, she moans, pressing her arse against my erection. Turning in my embrace, she looks up at me—water cascading over her—and kisses me hard, taking my breath away.

Deepening the kiss, her pussy rubs against my dick, and with one slight movement, I enter her. Slamming our bodies together, she moans against my lips before pulling back.

"Mmm, Chad, please," she begs huskily.

I chuckle softly, withdrawing my dick from her pussy and replacing it with two fingers. She hisses out a moan of pleasure when my fingers press against her sweet spot. And tipping her head back she arches her hips to ride my fingers. My eyes are locked on her body. I could get off just from watching Rox in pleasure without even touching myself. It's the sexiest fucking sight on the planet.

"Fuck, Chad. God, that feels so good," she moans out the words, biting down on her lip and looking straight at me when she careens over the edge with a shattering orgasm.

"Watching you come is the sexiest fucking sight ever, Rox," I tease, taking out my fingers and slipping them between my lips to lick them clean. I moan, staring at her and she shivers, both in pleasure, coming down from her orgasm and because the water has run cold.

Turning off the taps, she laughs softly, looking back at me whilst she gets out of the shower.

"I love you so fucking much, Chad."

"Back at you, sexy. Go get dressed. I'll meet you in the kitchen when you're ready."

She giggles, wrapping a towel around her perfect body before she walks across the hallway to her old room.

She still has some of her clothes in the wardrobe in there, even though since moving back in with me, she's slept in my room. We've barely had a night in the past month when we haven't made each other scream out in pleasure. I can't get enough of her, and I don't want to.

I'm feeling giddy and nervous as all hell.

Heading back to my room, I try to take my time getting dressed to calm my nerves. It doesn't really help, but I at least look dapper in black jeans and a white button-down shirt. I've left a few of the button's undone, and rolled the sleeves up to my elbows. I leave it untucked and slather on some of my fave cologne. I grab the small box, tucking it in the pocket of my jeans with my wallet, and head out to the kitchen to wait for Rox to be ready.

I'm shuffling on my feet, pacing the kitchen anxiously and when Rox comes out from the bathroom, I practically cream my daks on the spot and just about die.

My girl is stunning, an absolute fucking knockout in a mid-thigh, tight as hell, long-sleeved red dress with a square neckline that shows off her cleavage.

Still my Girl

I'm gaping at her, and she does a spin on her tiptoes in her red patent ballet flats to match the dress.

"You like baby? Sexy enough?" she asks, with a teasing tone in her voice.

"Nah, fuck, Rox. You're a knockout baby."

"Good," she replies with a laugh, stepping closer to me. It's then I take in the makeup she's wearing, smoky eyes, mascara on her lashes and strawberry-scented lip gloss. Rox is gorgeous without a speck of makeup, but with some, her beauty is only enhanced.

She's right up against me now—her lips a breath from mine—inhaling my cologne. "And you smell and look so handsome baby," she taunts.

I inhale her perfume—sweet and spicy—before crashing my lips against hers. She moans, practically jumping into my arms when I pull her closer. I know we need to go for our dinner reservation, but breaking the kiss and glancing at my watch confirms we can take a bit longer in leaving. Stepping closer to Rox again, I back us towards the kitchen counter.

"So Roxanne, what are you wearing under this tight red dress?"

She leans in, her breath fanning against my ear when she exhales and whispers, "Nothing."

"Mmm, fuck, baby," I curse, smashing my lips to hers again, grabbing her by the waist and hoisting her up to sit on the edge of the counter.

Breaking the kiss, I look down to see her dress has hitched up and her pussy is on full display, ready for me, glistening with her arousal. "Tell me what you want, baby," I tease. "Fuck me, Chad," she taunts, a seductive sexy smirk on her face. I groan, kissing her again, and her hands roam up under my untucked shirt, before effortlessly undoing my jeans. My dick is painfully hard, peeking out of my boxers, and breaking the kiss Rox glares down at it when I slip it out over the elastic of my boxers, slipping them down my arse a little.

"Spread your legs, baby," I demand, my eyes locked on hers. And as always she obeys. It turns me on so bad, and again taking her lips with mine in a fierce kiss I slam inside her, wrapping my arms around her waist. My thrusts are hard, fast and deep. And she moans loudly, cursing, "Fuck, fuck, oh Chad, fuck, so good."

Her dirty words entice me more, and I stop a moment, still inside her. "I love you, Roxanne Genevieve Donaghey. Come with me and tell me you love me."

I again rock my pelvis against hers, our bodies slamming against each other and I feel her pussy starting to clench around my dick. She's starting to tremble and shake, and I fill her with my load in a rush as she crashes down with me, calling out, "Oh my god, Chad Tristan Matthews, I love you!"

Still my Girl

Pulling out she's still trembling from her release, and I kiss her softly. "I think I want to make you come for the rest of your life Rox if it's that fucking good every time."

She doesn't say anything about my odd statement, just smirks at me and jeers, "So are we going out or did I just get dressed up to fuck you on the kitchen counter?"

I laugh, taking her hand and helping her jump down off the counter. She smooths her dress down, and I pull up my boxers and jeans. "We're going out, and we're late."

"Oh, ok, let's get going then. And you better drive, seeing as I drive like a snail."

"I think we need to get you a faster car," I tell her, taking her hand and leading her out.

With my other hand, I check that the little box is still in my back pocket—which thankfully it is—and I grab my phone and keys, whilst Rox grabs a small clutch.

"Ready, baby?" I ask as we head out to the Fiesta.

"I think so, but I don't know where we're going."

"It's a surprise baby, but you'll love it."

❤

Fifteen minutes later, I'm sliding into a carpark outside the restaurant and we race inside. Rox can't stop staring around at the fancy decor. And she's still smiling when we're seated at a table near the back.

In the middle is a lone candle and it flickers basking us both in soft light.

Caz May

"So, some drinks for the lovely couple to start?" the waiter asks.

I grab the wine menu, glancing at it and quickly deciding on a bottle.

"We'll have a bottle of the Barossa Valley vintage shiraz. And some bruschetta for entree thank you."

"Not a problem. I'll be back to take your order."

I take Rox's hand with mine across the table.

"You ok baby? You've gone all quiet on me."

"This place seems expensive Chad. Definitely one of the fanciest Lygon Street restaurants."

"Well, my treat baby. And tonight is special."

She smiles at me, making my heart gallop in my chest.

I love this girl so much it hurts, but it's also the best feeling in the world.

The waiter comes back with our wine and bruschetta. We order mains, Rox ordering Lasagna and me, chicken parmigiana.

The meals come quickly and we barely have time to chat before we're devouring the food. It's definitely worth the price tag. I'm just about finished eating when my phone vibrates with an incoming text. Opening it I laugh at my foster brothers eager question and text back a reply.

Jairus: have you asked her yet?
Chad: no you dick. Later at the bar.
Jairus: oh right. Which bar you heading to?

Still my Girl

Chad: Star sing karaoke
Jairus: bro you're shitting me yeah?
Chad: no, are you still down for meeting up?
Jairus: I guess. Catch ya there.

Rox is taking the last bites of her food and smiles at me.
"Who was that?"
"My foster brother, Jairus."
"Oh yeah. He's the one who wants to play AFL yeah?"
"Yeah, he's a dufus. We don't see each other much anymore though."
"Why's that?"
"Life I guess."
"Yeah," she muses with a smile, dabbing her napkin at the corner of her lips.
I smile back, quickly finishing my food. Our plates are cleared moments later, and I pay the bill before we head back out to the car.

It's a short drive to the karaoke bar and the smile that graces Rox's face when we get there makes my heart swell with love for her. Granted it's still hammering in my chest because I'm so damn nervous, which is also why I barely spoke to her at dinner.
I'm so afraid she's going to say no because we're in public, but I shove those thoughts aside to quell the nervousness and holding her hand with mine I pull her up to the bar

with me. I'm not letting my girl out of my sight in her sexy as sin red dress.

Some wanker would think he could have her, just like that Andy fucker did, and Rox is my girl, hopefully forever my girl in less than an hour.

I order her fave drink—the frozen strawberry daiquiri—and a light beer for myself. I still have to drive home at some point and I don't want our night ruined with a drunk driving charge.

Heading over to a booth with our drinks in hand, I nearly slosh my beer all over my shirt when someone slaps me on the back. I turn to find my idiot brother standing next to Rox.

"Hey bro," he greets me with a laugh, eyeing Rox whilst I eye the brunette standing next to him.

"Hi, Jairus," I greet him, giving him dagger eyes for the look in his eyes that's falling to Rox's cleavage. "And who's this?"

The girl on his arm smiles at me and says softly, "Hi, I'm Sara. Jairus' girlfriend."

I slap Jairus playfully on the arm.

"You fucker, you didn't tell me you had a girlfriend."

"It's new. Only met her recently, and didn't wanna jinx things. You know me."

"Yeah," I reply, laughing, and looking at Sara. "Hold on tight with this one, Sara. He's a good guy but likes to play the field."

Still my Girl

"Thanks," she replies, biting down on her lip.

"So, Roxanne Donaghey, you're looking good. How long has it been?" Jairus asks Rox, again giving her the once over with his green eyes.

"Um, I don't know. Years," Rox replies nervously.

I wanna slap my brother. He's got his girl standing next to him, and he still can't stop looking elsewhere.

Always a player, on and off the field.

"Bro, why don't we get you and your girl a drink? And let the girls get to know each other?"

I feel a little wary leaving Rox alone, but I need a moment with my brother.

Rox and Sara head over to a booth, sitting down and starting to chat, their eyes on us whilst we head back to the bar.

Jairus orders a whiskey, leaning back on the bar to gulp it down.

"Spill, Jairus," I jeer at him.

"Nothing to spill. Picked her up like a couple of months ago when I was out for the draft pick celebrations. And she's a ripper kisser and an even better root."

"Right. But you're not one to keep hitting the same girl."

"Yeah, but I'm trying to turn over a new leaf. Don't wanna get into the league and be known for my rep."

"Fair enough," I reply, gulping down the last mouthfuls of my beer.

"So, proposing huh?" he says, both of us looking over at the girls.

"Yeah, Rox has always been my girl. And everything with her is amazing."

"I'm glad, bro. I can only hope to find that kinda love."

"You will," I reply, heading back across the bar to the girls. "And you need to go see Mama or at least speak to her. She's missing you."

"I know. But life you know," he says more as a statement than a question.

I nod, giving Rox a kiss on the forehead and sitting down next to her whilst Jairus slides in next to Sara.

"So, you girls besties yet?" Jairus jeers.

"No, but we were talking about you," Rox replies laughing.

"Good things I hope," Jairus jeers again, with a wink.

He really makes me want to slap him. His cockiness is a big part of the reason I hardly ever see him. He always makes me fume at him, and want to knock some sense into him.

"Nah, very, very bad things, " Sara teases, which makes Jairus turn to her, kissing her in a full-on PDA that makes me want to puke.

"Bro, please. My fucking eyes."

He tears his lips from Sara's. "Sorry, bro. You know me."

"Unfortunately," I reply laughing.

The band has stopped playing and the first karaoke singer has stepped up to sing. I can feel the little box still burning a hole in my pocket. And I know it's now or never.

Still my Girl

Sliding out of the booth, I excuse myself, "Be right back. Gonna go line up to sing the next song."

"No worries," Jairus replies, winking at me.

Sara nods at me, and I again kiss Rox on the forehead.

Asking for the instrumental version of 'Marry me' by Train at the DJ booth makes my heart palpitate harder in my chest. I'm really fucking doing this.

The last singer suddenly finishes and I don't have time to go back to the booth, so quickly ask the DJ to announce for Rox to come up to the front of the stage. I step up onto the stage, clutching the microphone in my fist, and I close my eyes a moment, waiting.

"So for this next song, by special request I've been told there's a girl here by the name of Roxanne Donaghey. Roxanne if you're out there, Chad, would like you to come up the front of the stage to sing you a special song."

My eyes are still closed, and the crowd is chanting Roxanne, clapping wildly just like the wild beating of my heart.

"Oh and here she is, red dress and all. Give her a big hand, all."

The crowd again erupts, and I open my eyes, looking down at Rox in front of me as the first chords of the song start to play.

I start to sing the words, the first lyrics flowing out of my mouth softly, and I smile through them when I get to the *'Marry me, Today and every day, Marry me,'* part.

I continue singing, my eyes locked on Rox the whole time until I get to the final marry me part and I take the box from my pocket, dropping to my knee on the stage, singing out the final words, *"Say you will, mm-hmm, Say you will, Mm-hmm, Marry me, Roxanne?"*

The song ends and Rox is up on the stage with me, the biggest smile on her face.

"Yes, Chad, oh my god, yes I will marry you."

I slide the simple solitaire diamond ring on her finger and stand up—dropping the microphone to the floor—kissing her hard.

Cheering and clapping erupt around us, and I'm beyond elated. Breaking the kiss I smile at her. "I love you, Roxanne Genevieve Donaghey. You're my girl and I can't wait until you're my wife."

"I love you to Chad Tristan Matthews, and I'm always yours." I hug her tightly, lifting her feet off the floor for a moment.

"Well, that was a bit of excitement for the night. Congrats to the gorgeous couple," the DJ announces as I lead Rox off the stage.

Back at the booth Jairus and Sara hug us both in congratulations. And we say goodbye to them. I'm more than ready to head home and celebrate being engaged to Rox; naked and just us.

Epilogue. Chad

6 months later

My heart is hammering in my chest, standing under the arch at the beach with Jessie by my side. I considered asking Jairus to be my best man, but he was too busy with some footy related thing or so he told me. We've not talked much since I proposed to Rox six months ago, and I kinda miss my dufus younger brother.

Jessie elbows me. "You ok, Chadster?"

"Yeah, just nervous."

"Trust me, once you see her you'll be fine."

I turn to look at him, smiling. "Really? Is that how it was with you and Teags? You didn't seem nervous."

"Trust me. I was shitting bricks."

"Yeah, that about sums it up," I jeer laughing. He pats me on the back and nods towards his wife Teagan sitting in the front row, her pregnant belly showing in her tight dress.

Still my Girl

"Just think of the wedding night," Jessie says, out of character considering I'm marrying his younger sister. "Will do Jessman, but I'll spare you the details."

"You better, Chadster," he jeers laughing and then smiling when the music 'I get to love you' by Ruelle starts to play from the portable speakers.

Looking to the end of the rose petal aisle I see Nellie, Rox's best friend—the maid of honour—has started to walk towards us. She looks pretty with her chestnut hair down —brushing her shoulders—and a royal blue strapless dress that swishes the sand at her feet.

She steps up to me at the front of the aisle and kisses me on the cheek, whispering to me, "She looks stunning."

I shift on my bare feet, squishing the sand between my toes, and snapping my fingers in my suspenders before I turn to the end of the aisle and see my girl.

And Nellie was right. Rox looks stunning, utterly breathtaking in a strapless dress that hugs her delicious sexy curves, before flaring out at the back. She's holding a simple bouquet of white and pink roses and her smile is wide, her hair curled into ringlets that bounce as she walks towards me.

My heart is hammering even harder in my chest, in anxiousness but excitement. My dick is threatening to make a spectacle in my slacks, but I mentally tell it to calm down when Rox steps up to me. Her Dad smiles at me.

"Take care of her son," he says softly.

"I will, Mr Donaghey," I reply, taking Rox's hand with mine when she hands her bouquet to Nellie.

I nod to the celebrant to begin the ceremony. He nods, smiling at us both.

"Friends and family, we're gathered here today to share in the love of Chad Tristan Matthews and Roxanne Genevieve Donaghey. They share a love that is deep, special and lifelong and it is my pleasure to marry them. Chad, do you take Roxanne to be your wife?"

"I do, I so do," I declare happily.

"Roxanne, do you take Chad to be your husband?"

Rox replies sweetly, "Yes, I do."

"Chad will you now share the vows you've prepared for Roxanne."

I squeeze Rox's hand, looking straight at her.

"Rox, I love you with my whole damn heart. There's never been a day that you were not my girl, and you are and always will be my girl. I promise not another day will go by without you knowing how much you mean to me, and no matter what life throws at us, you're still my girl, forever."

She smiles sweetly at me. "Aww, Chad, I love you with my whole heart to. And there's nothing more I want than to be your girl. I promise to make you feel how much I love you, forever."

Cheekily, I press a kiss to her cheek, and the celebrant and our guests laugh. "Now that the couple has shared their vows with each other, they will now exchange rings to symbolise the commitment and promise they've made to one another today," he says, nodding to Jessie.

He hands me the rings from his pocket, two matching yellow gold bands.

The celebrant continues," Chad as you place this ring on Roxanne's finger, repeat these words after me, 'This ring is a symbol of my love for you and the promise we made today.' "

I repeat the words, sliding the ring onto Rox's finger, making her smile and giggle.

"Roxanne, as you place this ring on Chad's finger, repeat these words after me,'This ring is a symbol of my love for you and the promise we made today.' "

Rox repeats the words, sliding the ring onto my finger.

All I want now is to make things official.

"Chad and Roxanne, now that you have declared your love together in matrimony, and have promised yourselves to each other through vows and by the giving of rings, and have declared your intent before God and your family and friends, it is my pleasure to pronounce you husband and wife. Chad, you may kiss your Bride."

And that I do, grabbing Rox around the waist, crashing my lips to hers and dipping her down in a passionate kiss that makes our guests cheer and applaud.

"Ladies and Gentlemen, it is my delight to introduce to you for the very first time, Mr and Mrs Chad and Roxanne Matthews."

I take Rox's hand in mine, and we head over to the small table by the arch to quickly complete the signing of the register before we head down the aisle to be congratulated by our family and friends.

I've never been happier. All I can hope for now is for Rox to forever be my girl.

Epilogue. Roxanne

Two years later

As we do every fourth Sunday of the month we're having a family barbecue at our house. Thankfully the weather is warm, but not hot for a November arvo.

Standing on the back deck I'm watching my hubby and my brother playing with our toddlers. My brother is chasing his daughter Aurora around, but the look on his face is forlorn. Chad is giving our son Channing a piggyback and I can practically hear Channing's giggles from the other side of the backyard.

Nellie comes outside, standing beside me and following my gaze.

"How's Jessie doing?" she asks, an odd almost smile at the corner of her mouth.

I look to my best friend, and reply, "He's coping but I can tell he's struggling."

Nellie nods. "Yeah, it's so sad for him. I can't believe she cheated on him again."

"I know. He never should have married her, but love does make us do crazy things."

"Yeah, I'll go and tell them everything is ready and get the kids inside to wash up."

"Thanks, Nel."

I watch my best friend walking over to my brother, noticing the way she smiles at him, but ignores Chad completely like he's invisible. He wanders over to me, smiling.

"Hey, wife. You ok? You look sexy but exhausted."

"Well, thanks, but yeah, I am exhausted. It's hard dealing with Channing and growing twins in my belly."

He kisses my belly. And then my lips, softly but emotion-charged.

"I'll pamper you tonight, baby," he tells me with his sexy signature doubled dimpled smirk.

"Sounds great. And maybe some hot dirty sex to?"

"I'm always up for hot dirty sex with you."

"I'm so glad I'm your girl Chad Matthews. I love you."

"You'll always be my girl, Roxanne Matthews. I love you too."

I definitely couldn't be happier with how things have turned out. Our lives have changed so much in the last couple of years, but I've never felt happier. I give Chad a hot kiss, forgetting for a moment that we're outside until Nellie jeers, "Eww you two, get a damn room."

Still my Girl

She has Channing on her hip and Jessie is behind walking towards us holding Aurora's hand. "There are children around," Nellie says laughing.

I look at Chad laughing. He smiles when I reply to Nellie, "Children who know how much love is in their lives, so aren't immune to seeing their parents and family show that love."

"Yeah, so very true," Chad says as we all head inside to eat.

Sitting down at the table, I look at my brother whilst I'm piling food onto a plate to pass to Channing who is sitting next to me. I can't help but wonder if something is going on between Nellie and him from the way they're looking at each other, stealing glances at each other and smiling.

After all the crap my brother has been through with his divorce and having to cope with being a single dad because his stupid ex-wife cheated and wanted nothing to do with her kid, I hope my brother can find his girl and find love and happiness just like I have with Chad.

And it makes me a little excited to think that my best friend could be his girl. I've always wanted a sister. And I'm hoping that dreams all really do come true because most of mine have.

The End
(Or is it?)

Australian Slang Glossary

Ute-Truck

Bludger- someone lazy, doesn't do much and possibly relies on social security benefits

Ripper- something really good/great

Ridgy-Didge- Cool

Bonzer-Great, awesome

Pash/ing/ed- to kiss/make out

Arvo- afternoon

Chunder- Vomit, throw up

Gobby- Blowjob

Aussie Kiss- going down on a girl

Daks- pants/trousers/underwear

Undies/Knickers/Jocks-underwear (female knickers, male Jocks, undies both)

Dakking/ed- to pull or have pulled someone daks down (see above)

Bathers- universal name for female swimwear

Budgie Smugglers- small male swimmer that looks like underwear (google this one to see)

Thongs- Footwear, otherwise known as flip flops

Esky- Cooler-you keep drinks cool in it

Dunny- toilet

Bogan-white trash/trailer trash

Old Fella- Your father/Dad

Franger- Condom, Trojan etc

Milo- a malt chocolate powered drink mix (can be made hot or cold)

Macca's-MacDonalds

Still my Girl

Fair Dinkum- used to emphasise or seek confirmation of the genuineness or truth of something

Fucking/Bloody oath- similar to above, but an extreme or emphasised way of saying yes.

Shark Week/Rags- A woman's monthly cycle

Stuffed if I know- a nicer way to say fucked if I know

AFL- Australian Rules Football

Playlist

Below is the playlist of songs for this story. They're in particular order. The Spotify playlist link is at the bottom.

1. Still My Girl-Jon McLaughlin
2. Only One-Ali Gatie
3. I Won't Lie-Go Radio
4. Old Me-5SOS
5. Didn't I-One Republic
6. Our Love-Incubus
7. Physical-Dua Lipa
8. What If I Told You I Love You-Ali Gatie
9. If You Could Only See-Tonic
10. I Get To Love You-Ruelle
11. Drown-Martin Garrix ft Clinton Kane
12. Run-Matt Nathanson/Sugarland
13. Come on get higher-Matt Nathanson
14. Must be another way (acoustic)- Nick Frandiani
15. Marry me-Train

About the Author

Caz May is a librarian/teacher by trade, but was always destined to be an author from a young age.

In her spare time, she can be found devouring books or writing her own stories with characters that may not be the typical romance heroes but are loveable just as much.

Caz is married to her own real-life bearded hero and has two fur babies.

She lives for Iced coffee, especially from Gloria Jeans or a Farmers Union but pretty much just loves food in general.

When she's not writing, or reading a book most likely she can probably be found asleep or binge-watching shows on Netflix and Stan. And probably also drooling over her character inspiration on Instagram as well.

Check out her Instagram or other socials to get in touch.

Instagram- @cazmayauthor

Facebook- @CazMayAuthor

BookBub-Caz May https://www.bookbub.com/profile/caz-may

Spotify- cazcat25

Website- https://cazcat25.wixsite.com/cazmay-author

Goodreads https://www.goodreads.com/cazmay

Acknowledgments

Hey lovely readers!

I can't believe another book is done. I've really enjoyed writing this one, and honestly I don't know who to thank, but each and every one of you that has taken a chance on my books.

If you've enjoyed this story, then please review on Amazon (QR code below) and any other platforms you can.

And if you haven't read Jairus' story Roommates Don't Kiss & Tell (Bk 1 of Always Only You), read on for a preview and check it out on Amazon by clicking the below QR Code.

Thanks again to all of you!

I love you all and appreciate each and every one of you!

Signing off! For now!

Caz May xx

Roommates Don't Kiss & Tell Preview

Prologue

Late December 2014

I was what most people would describe as a plain Jane, not beautiful, maybe cute, painfully shy and a late bloomer in every way.

It wasn't as though I didn't think about guys, or didn't want to kiss someone, but meek, petite Annika didn't register on their radars.

Caz May

Instead they all went after the girls who somehow over the summer holidays grew voluptuous breasts and looked as though they'd gotten butt implants.

There was only one guy I'd wanted all through high school, watching him from afar, as he dated nearly every girl in our year level.

He had the boyish good looks every girl lusted over, his fiery red hair unruly and his dark eyes that made every girl swoon including myself.

What was odd about Austin though, was he was a certified geek; academically a science whiz and totally addicted to video games.

If he wasn't buried in a book or glued to the television screen, he was pashing his latest hussy.

It was stupid and incredibly naive to want to be Austin Belvinz's girlfriend, as even though I was nerdy I wasn't exactly his usual type.

He always preferred brunettes and the aforementioned curvy girls, not little old me, blonde haired, no curves at all and so shy I'd barely spoken two words to anyone let alone a guy.

I spent my days in the library, my nose buried in a book hiding down the back of the shelves where no one would disturb me, or so I thought.

Until the biggest storm Stawell had seen rolled in turning day into night.

Still my Girl

The lights flicker, and every person in the library screams like the end of the world is descending upon us. When they cut out completely, an eerie calm settles over the library.

Liking the darkness, I sigh, taking my phone out of my pocket and shining the torchlight onto my page to continue reading.

Around me, I can hear faint whispers and the sound of lips puckering as someone is pashing nearby.

Feet shuffle along the gap between the shelves. A tall guy who isn't thinking about where he's going holds a torchlight up scanning the shelves to find an item. He falls on top of me in a tangled heap when he bumps into my feet.

Holding up my torch to see, my face is now only a whisper away from Austin's.

"Sorry, I couldn't see," he says apologetically, stating the obvious.

"Um...well..." I stammer, completely tongue tied as he stares at me, not seeming like he was going to move anytime soon.

My heart is pounding, having him so close and speaking to me.

"It's Annika yeah?" he asks, shocking me that he actually knows my name, even though I'd spent Christmas at his house for the last few years with my family.

Caz May

I'd been so painfully shy, even as a sixteen-year-old that I'd stayed glued to my Mum's side and didn't engage with him at all.

"Yes," I manage to squeeze out from my pursed lips.

"Well, Annika," he states, climbing off my lap and sitting next to me stretching out his legs in front of him, crossing them at the ankles, "I'm Austin. Nice to officially meet you, even though I've known you for years," he coos, with a hint of laughter in his tone.

Gulping, I will my mind to cooperate with my tongue to actually say more than two words to the gorgeous guy sitting next to me.

No doubt he looked dapper as hell like he always did, wearing skin-tight dark jeans, a white second skin t-shirt and his purple Nikes.

In the darkness I could feel his eyes on me, like he had cat like night vision. His hand brushes against mine, and he laces our fingers together, breaking the silence when he whispers, "I always wanted to talk to you, but didn't have the guts."

I chuckle softly, completely taken aback by his confession, but even more taken aback when I feel his rough hand across my cheek, his finger grazing across my bottom lip.

He inhales a breath, and lets it out desperately, before pressing his lips to mine.

Still my Girl

His kiss soft, his lips warm and tingly on mine. My heart is galloping in my chest, my mind screaming 'your first kiss, Anni, your first kiss is with Austin, you lucky bitch'

Wanting more I gasp, and feel him smile as he pulls away. The lights flickering back on cause everyone in the library to hiss in appreciation.

Austin was still looking at me, and I feel my cheeks turning crimson.

"I guess you liked that," he jeers at me light-heartedly.

Not trusting myself to speak, I nod and gape when he asks, "Will you go out with me on Saturday?"

Work brain, say yes Anni, Austin is asking you out, what are you waiting for?

"Yes, Austin," I reply smiling.

"Great, meet me at Clocktower at five?"

"Ok," I reply, trying to not sound too eager, as he stands up, brushing his hands across his butt to wipe off the dirt from the floor.

"See you then Anni," he coos, making my heart skip at his use of my nickname.

Shutting my book, I hold it to my chest, hoping that finally my luck had turned and I was going to be Austin's girlfriend.

I'd most certainly dreamt about it, just as I had dreamt about kissing him and his kiss was far beyond anything I could have dreamt of.

Caz May

One | Monopoly Night

Two- and a-bit years later
May 2017

Sitting cross legged on the fluffy rug, the fireplace
in our Richmond apartment is ablaze warming my
back and making me feel comfortably warm
enough to only be wearing three-quarter leggings
and a V-neck fitted t-shirt in late May.
Across from me on the other side of the low glass
coffee table, Austin is sitting with his long legs
outstretched, wearing a tank top that shows his
defined arms with pyjama pants that hang low on
his hips, pooling at his crotch.
Gazing at his outfit I have to stop myself from
licking my lips, and jumping him.
He might have been my best friend now, but I
can't deny his good looks and the attraction to
him I still feel.
I certainly wasn't in love with him anymore
though, our breakup amicable as we both
thought we were better off as friends.
For some reason, if we defined what we had
together as boyfriend and girlfriend we fought

Still my Girl

like cats and dogs, never kissed and certainly
never had sex.

Austin had been my first kiss, and I'd been
shocked when we slept together that I was his
first time too, as he was mine.

It had crossed my mind that it was maybe the
reason that he couldn't now let go of being with
me completely, preferring to be my best friend
and partake in some bedroom action when he
saw fit.

Sometimes I hated myself for giving in, but sex
with Austin was good; not that I had anything to
compare to.

I also knew since moving to Melbourne for
University, finding the two-bedroom apartment
we now called home together that I'd not been
the only girl Austin had snuggled up with
between the sheets.

Me on the other hand, romance wasn't really on
my radar, too busy with my nursing degree and
knowing that if I really did want sex, Austin would
be more than willing to help me scratch the itch.

Part of me wondered if he did want us to get back
together, that maybe he was in denial about how
he felt about me. He'd never actually said I love
you when we were together, only since we'd
crossed back into the friend zone and his tone
was always jovial whenever the word 'love'' came
out of his mouth.

Caz May

I shake myself back to reality, gazing at him sitting across from me. He bites down on his lip, concentrating as he shakes the dice in his hand, no doubt wishing in his mind to roll a six to get out of jail for the fifth time since we'd started our usual Thursday night game of Monopoly.

Throwing it against the board, it teetered a little before stopping with four as the number facing up.

I laugh at his response, "Fuck a duck, I suck at this game."

"Yeah says the guy who owns half the board right now."

"You're just upset because you have to pay me big bucks when you land on my squares," he jeers taking a puff of his joint.

My eyes dart from the rolled paper to his eyes, "Why do you have to smoke that inside Aust? The place reeks of weed and we've got the inspection on Monday."

He laughs, stabbing the stubby remains in the ashtray on the edge of the coffee table, "Sorry, Mum, didn't know it was a crime to smoke a joint in my own house," he chastises me, knowing how much I hate when he calls me 'Mum'.

"Um, actually, Austin. It is a crime and something that could get us kicked out of here."

Picking up the dice for my turn, I scowl at him, knowing my comment is falling on deaf ears. The

Still my Girl

only reason I even really cared about Austin's weed habit was because I'd seen it become a gateway drug with my older brother, before he took to Meth and Cocaine. His battle with addiction partly being what led me to nursing, wanting to specialise in drug rehabilitation. Seeing the look on my face as I throw the dice against the board Austin breaks the silence, "Babe you need to lighten up, it wouldn't kill you to take a drag once in awhile."

"Not going to happen Aust and you know why." The dice crashes against his ashtray, with only two facing up, the expression on his face changes to a frown, "Sorry Anni, I shouldn't have said that. I miss Alex too, but it wouldn't hurt you to lighten up a little."

"I know, Aust, I'll try ok?" I promise, moving my koala pawn two spaces along the board, only to find I'd landed on the one square of the board he'd bought up big on. He had it lined with hotels, and I scoff as I count the paper money I need to hand over to him.

Holding the wad of paper money in my hand out towards him, he shakes his head laughing, "Pay up babe."

"Here, take it all bitch," I laugh, quoting one of our favourite movies 'Centre Stage'.

Again, shaking his head, he taps a finger against his cheek, "Uh-uh...pay up babe.... I don't want your wad of paper cash."

"Oh, so that's how it is huh?" I tease, smirking at him.

"Tease me like that babe, and you'll pay with a proper pash."

I curse myself that my insides flip-flop at his cheeky suggestion.

"So are you paying up or not babe?" He taunts leaning across the coffee table.

Leaning forward I close my eyes, leaning closer to him to press a kiss to his cheek, but instead I feel his lips on mine.

He pulls back, "Anni, you could have just jumped me babe," he laughs.

"I...I didn't want to kiss you Aust," I protest, cursing myself for the blush that is rising up my cheeks.

"Your face says otherwise Anni," he teases, licking his lips, "so...you have two minutes to get away or I'll fuck you right here in front of the fire," he threatens with a teasing tone.

Go on Anni, you need sex girl, you've been so uptight lately

I hate that my subconscious is right, but it is, my vibrator just isn't cutting it and Austin was offering as usual, a quickie.

Still my Girl

I toy for a moment, of letting him take me on the fluffy rug by the fireplace, but I know it's a bad idea as our new roommate is supposed to be arriving sometime today and he hasn't turned up yet.

I wasn't shy around Austin anymore, even when it came to sex but I certainly didn't want a stranger to walk in on our romp to meet me for the first time with my daks around my feet.

Giggling I get to my feet, turning to look back at him when I stand in the doorway of his bedroom, beckoning him with a finger and a smirk.

Before I even have a moment to think about the fact that I'm teasing my best friend he's in front of me, grabbing me by the waist and carrying me to his single bed.

Smashing a kiss to my lips, he moans a little.

I can feel his dick straining against the front of his pyjama pants, pressing against my stomach.

"God Anni, you're such a tease," he drawls.

"Really? I didn't do anything," I laugh, as he reaches over to the drawers beside the bed to grab a condom out.

At the same time, we both yank our daks to our ankles, and I giggle as he rolls the condom on.

Smashing another kiss to my lips, he drives himself inside me, hissing against my lips as I rise my hips to meet his.

Caz May

Hearing a banging sound, I break our kiss, my eyes locking on the door that is still slightly ajar. Gasping at what I see in the doorway, I push Austin off my body.

Both of us struggle to pull up our daks, the voice of the figure standing in the doorway speaks, "Sorry to interrupt ya romp, but I'm your new roomie, Jairus."

My cheeks flush, as I look at the floor racing out of Austin's room to my own. Slamming the door shut I flop down on my double bed, feeling utterly humiliated and downright stupid that I'd not told Austin to shut the door.

I might as well have been naked, as my new roommate had just seen a lot more than he needed to.

How in the hell am I going to face my hot new roommate now?

Still my Girl

www.ingramcontent.com/pod-product-compliance
Lightning Source LLC
Chambersburg PA
CBHW030429120726
47903CB00003B/878